P9-AGE-197
Volume I

W.I.T.C.H.

Will Irma Taranee Cornelia Hay Lin

Part x.
Ladies vs. W.I.T.C.H.
Volume 1

CONTENTS

118

All in a Day's Work

IT'S 7 A.M...
A LOT OF ALARM CLOCKS ARE GOING OFF IN HEATHERFIELD...
BZZZZ
BZZ
BZZ
BZZZZ
BZZZ
...INCLUDING CORNELIA'S!
BZ-BZ
BZ-BZ
BZ-BZ
AAARGH!
BTUMP
BZ-BZ
BZ-BZ
BZ-BZ

DIDN'T I DECIDE TO GET A NEW ALARM CLOCK?
BZ-BZ
BZ-BZ
BZ-BZ
SLAM
DECIDE?! OF COURSE, HOW COULD I FORGET...?
I MADE A TON OF DECISIONS ABOUT MY FUTURE YESTERDAY!
HOW ABOUT SLEEPING IN A BIT LONGER? IN MY FUTURE, I'M TIRED!
LILIAN? WHAT ARE YOU DOING HERE?
I WAS SCARED OF THE DARK...
BUT YOU'RE NOT SCARED OF THE DARK.
UM...OF SPIDERS?

YOU KNOW WHAT? IT'S NO PROBLEM! ONE OF THE DECISIONS I MADE YESTERDAY WAS...TO IMPROVE MY RELATIONSHIP WITH MY FAMILY!
MEAN-ING?
MEANING I'LL BE NICER TO YOU, MOM, AND DAD.
BUT YOU'RE ALREADY NICE... KINDA.
THANKS! STILL, I'D LIKE TO DO BETTER.
THEN YOU CAN TIDY MY ROOM AND GET ME ICE CREAM FOR BREAKFAST, YEAH?
WHY NOT? BUT LET ME GO OVER WHAT ELSE I WANT TO DO.
MOOOOM!
CORNELIA'S BEING WEIRD!
YOU SHOULD SEE YOUR DAD...
HUH?

SO...FROM NOW ON, I WANT TO—
Improve my relationships with my loved ones!
Learn to apologize!
Become a math genius!
Start exercising in the afternoons!
Study French!
Be less obsessed with my appearance!
THAT WILL BE TOUGH.

LET'S START WITH...
Improve Relationships: Difficulty Level 5
~YAWN~ CAN SOMEONE PASS THE JELLY?
HERE, DADDY.
DADDY?
DO YOU WANT SOME CEREAL TOO, DADDY-O?
CEREAL? DADDY-O?
AND YOU, MOMMY? HOW ABOUT SOME ORANGE JUICE?
MOMMY? ORANGE JUICE?
YOUR ICE CREAM WILL BE RIGHT OUT, SIS.
MOM! CORNELIA'S STILL BEING WEIRD.

DING
OH, TOAST'S READY FOR MOMMY AND DADDY-O.
What's this about...?
She's up to something...
CORNELIA...
HOW MAY I HELP YOU?
IS THERE SOMETHING YOU NEED TO TELL US?
NO.
YOU SURE?
WELL, THE TOAST'S A LITTLE BURNT...
...BUT I DID MY BEST!
SFRIZZLE
ER...I'M LATE! I'LL EAT AT THE CAFÉ.

SHORTLY AFTER...
THERE HAS TO BE SOMETHING I CAN DO FOR YOU!
WELL, YOU CAN TAKE THE TRASH OUT.
I MEAN SOMETHING *IMPORTANT*!
IT IS! I ***HATE*** TAKING OUT THE TRASH.
REALLY?
ABSOLUTELY.
THEN I'LL DO IT.
WOULD YOU LOOK AT THAT. YOU DON'T NEED TO DO MUCH TO FEEL USEFUL...
YUCK...I MIGHT LOSE MY SENSE OF SMELL, THOUGH...

I'B DOING IT, BOBBY! SHEE?
GOOD GIRL! IF YOU HURRY, YOU CAN GIVE IT DIRECTLY TO THE GARBAGEMEN.
SOWWY... BORE GARBAGE COBING...
?
WHAT A STRANGE... ACCENT?
UM...NO... I JUST...
AH, THE SMELL, HUH? YOU GET USED TO IT, YOU KNOW. I'VE GOT SOME TRICKS...
OH?
SNIFF
SURE. FOR INSTANCE, VIOLETS...
SNIFF
HERE.
OOH, THANK YOU.

LOOK! THE GARBAGE-MAN GAVE ME SOME FLOWERS!
HOW NICE.
WHAT NOW?
PUT THEM IN A VASE.
NO, I MEAN— WHAT ELSE CAN I DO FOR YOU?
YOU'RE IN A GOOD MOOD, HUH? WELL, THERE ARE SHIRTS TO IRON, THE ATTIC TO CLEAN, AND THE CAR NEEDS AN OIL CHANGE.
......
KIDDING...JUST SHIRTS TO IRON.
YAY!
WHAT A DOLL TODAY.
Improve Relationships: OKAY

WOW! I FEEL REALLY GOOD ABOUT MYSELF...
HEY! THERE'S SALT ON MY ICE CREAM.
I'LL DO BETTER NEXT TIME. BUT LET ME STILL GIVE YOU SOMETHING SWEET...
MWAH!
MOM! CORNELIA'S KISSING ME!
GOOD RESOLUTIONS EVEN MAKE ME FEEL...
... PRETTIER!
Be Less Obsessed with My Appearance!
THAT'S RIGHT! QUIT IT, CORNY.

BUT IT'S HARD. I'M SO USED TO STEALING A GLANCE EVERY NOW AND THEN...
...IN SHOP WINDOWS.
Be Less Obsessed with My...
ALL RIGHT, ALL RIGHT!
NEXT IS...
Learn to Apologize: Difficulty Level 10
ARGH! I CAN LEAVE THIS FOR LAST...
Learn to Apologize: Difficulty Level 10
OKAY, FINE...

I HAVE TO APOLOGIZE TO IRMA. I FORGOT TO WISH HER HAPPY BIRTHDAY!
LAIR
I DIDN'T GET HER A GIFT EITHER. AND THE NEXT DAY, WHEN I SAW HER AT SCHOOL...
"...I GAVE HER A FRIENDLY PAT ON THE SHOULDER."
BUMP
HEY, WHERE DID YOU FIND THAT DRESS? YOUR GRANDMA'S CLOSET?
NO, IT'S A PRESENT FROM MY MOM!
WHOOPS! WELL, I'VE SEEN WORSE.
SO HOW WAS YESTERDAY? I DIDN'T SEE YOU ALL DAY...
OH, IT WAS NOTHING SPECIAL... JUST HAD A LITTLE PARTY.
AND YOU DIDN'T INVITE ME?
OF COURSE I DID! TWO WEEKS AGO! WITH SCENTED NOTEPAPER!

THOUGH YOU DIDN'T MISS MUCH...IT WAS ONLY MY BIRTHDAY!
OH, IN THAT CASE...
YOUR WH-WH-WHAT?!
YOU KNOW, THAT PARTY YOU HAVE ONCE A YEAR WITH YOUR CLOSEST FRIENDS? THAT ONE!
THAT DAY WHEN EVERYONE MAKES YOU FEEL IMPORTANT? AND KEEPS YOU IN THEIR THOUGHTS? THAT ONE!
UGH! HOW EMBARRASSING! I STILL CRINGE THINKING ABOUT IT.
BUT I'LL MAKE IT UP TO HER. THE NEW CORNELIA KNOWS HOW TO APOLOGIZE.
LAIR
MAYBE TOMORROW, THOUGH!
!
Learn to Apologize: Difficulty Level 10
LAIR

OKAY, LET'S TAKE A DEEP BREATH AND DO IT...
GAH!
DRIIIIIIIN
CORNELIA! HEY! I WAS ABOUT TO LEAVE FOR SCHOOL.
UM, HI...
YOU'RE MAKING A WEIRD FACE. IS SOMETHING WRONG?
NO! I JUST CAME TO... TO...
...TOAPOLOGIZEFORNOTCOMING TOYOURBIRTHDAYPARTY!
HUH?
TO APOLOGIZE... ABOUT...YOUR BIRTHDAY...
OH, THAT! I'D FORGOTTEN ALL ABOUT IT.

REALLY? YOU DON'T HATE ME?
NO WAY! IN FACT, HANG ON—
I SAVED YOU A SLICE OF CAKE.
AWWW, THANKS!
SO GOOD... -MUNCH- YOU SEE, I HAD A LOT OF THINGS TO DO...
LIKE?
WELL... -CHOMP- DOING MY NAILS, GOING TO THE DRY CLEANERS'...
WOW, IMPORTANT STUFF.
THEN PETER CALLED ME AND...
CORNY, THIS ISN'T APOLOGIZING! THIS IS MAKING EXCUSES!
UM...RIGHT...ANYWAY, I'LL GET YOU A GIFT AS SOON AS I CAN.
GEE, THANKS.

HEY, I JUST WANTED TO SAY SORRY!
OH, REALLY? WELL, MAYBE YOU SHOULD LEARN HOW!
DIDN'T KNOW THIS WAS A LESSON.
SPEAKING OF... DID YOU REMEMBER TO BRING ME THE HISTORY NOTES?
OH NO!
I REALLY NEED THEM! I WAS GONNA GO OVER THEM IN OUR FREE PERIOD!
I'LL RUN BACK AND—
DON'T BOTHER. I'LL ASK A FRIEND.
OOF!
SLAM
WHAT A DISASTER...
Learn to Apologize:
TRY AGAIN

LATER, AT SCHOOL...
SIGH... IRMA HATES ME.
POISON
BUT I'LL FIX IT. NOW LET'S MOVE ON TO...
Become a Math Genius: Difficulty Level 10
THERE SHE IS! ENRIKA!
BRILLIANT, GORGEOUS, SUPER-NICE...
...AND THUS, OCCASIONALLY UNBEARABLE!
CORNELIA! WHAT'S WITH THAT LOOK? IS SOMETHING WRONG?

WELL, YES. I'VE GOT A PROBLEM... A MATH PROBLEM! MY GRADES HAVE BEEN TERRIBLE LATELY.
AND?
I WAS WONDERING IF YOU COULD GIVE ME SOME ADVICE...
HOW ARE YOU SO GOOD AT IT?
I'LL TELL YOU...BUT YOU HAVE TO TELL ME WHAT MAKES YOU SO *MYSTERIOUS*.
ME? MYSTERIOUS?
YEAH! IT ALWAYS SEEMS LIKE YOU'RE HIDING SOMETHING.
MAYBE BECAUSE I *AM*...
You know, I can do MAGIC!
I knew it!

I'VE GOT SPECIAL, UNBELIEVABLE POWERS.
ME TOO...
I KNOW, I KNOW! BUT APART FROM MATH...WHERE DO YOU BUY THAT NAIL POLISH?
BUY IT? I MAKE IT!
HOW?
I *MIX* THE COLORS. RED PLUS BLUE EQUALS PURPLE.
I SEE. SIMPLE BUT EFFECTIVE.
WOW! LOOK AT THAT GUY!
UM...I'M ALREADY TAKEN...
OKAY, THEN I'LL DESCRIBE HIM—TALL, EYES AS BLUE AS THE SKY...
...SANDY-BLOND HAIR...
I PREFER BRUNETTES.
THEN LET ME TELL YOU ABOUT HIS FRIEND.

DARK HAIR, SUPER-TALL, EYES THE COLOR OF HONEY...
?
HONEY? I'VE NEVER SEEN THAT BEFORE.
HA-HA! YOU LOOKED, MISS **TAKEN**.
THERE'S NO DARK-HAIRED DUDE! VERY FUNNY.
C'MON, REALLY...TELL ME WHAT MAKES YOU SO MYSTERIOUS.
I DID ALREADY— MAGIC.
AND?
BANGS OVER ONE EYE...
OH!
...OR BOTH! GO FOR A BEHIND-A-WATERFALL EFFECT.
SIMPLE BUT EFFECTIVE.

I SHOULD GET TO CLASS. SO ABOUT MATH...
START BY BELIEVING THAT YOU **CAN'T** MAKE MISTAKES.
WHAT?
YEAH! EQUATIONS, CALCULATIONS...THEY ONLY HAVE ONE ANSWER—THE **RIGHT** ONE!
THINK ABOUT IT...YOU JUST HAVE TO FOLLOW THE ROAD THAT LEADS TO THE SOLUTION.
BUT HOW DO I FIND IT?
FIRST OF ALL, BE CONFIDENT. TRY SOLVING THIS...
SEE YOU DURING RECESS!
O-OKAY...
BUT CAREFUL WITH THE BANGS. FOR MATH, YOU NEED TO KEEP BOTH EYES OPEN.

Become a Math Genius: OKAY, Even Though It'll Take a While...
But Make a New Friend: OKAY! 100 BONUS POINTS!
AT RECESS...
IS...IS IT CORRECT?
YUP! I KNEW YOU'D GET IT. YOU'RE GOOD.
AND YOU... I HAVE TO SAY—YOU'RE BRILLIANT, KIND, AND...
...UNBEARABLE, RIGHT?
NOT AT ALL! MAYBE YOU ALSO KNOW HOW TO SAY SORRY AFTER LETTING A FRIEND DOWN?
WELL, IT CAN BE HARD...
...BUT I USUALLY APOLOGIZE AND THEN SHUT MY MOUTH. SAYING ANYTHING MORE COULD...
...RUIN EVERYTHING. YES, I KNOW.

THAT AFTERNOON...
Exercise: Difficulty Level 5
BREATHABLE-FABRIC CLOTHES, RUNNING SHOES, AND A FITNESS TRACKER!
HEY, NOT BAD...
Be Less Obsessed with My Appearance!
RIGHT! LET'S FOCUS.

LET'S GO!
I'LL JOG FOR TWO MINUTES, THEN SPRINT AS FAST AS I CAN FOR THIRTY SECONDS.
Well done! Excellent rhythm!
THANKS.
HUFF, HUFF!
FUNNY, I DIDN'T THINK TWO MINUTES WAS SO LONG.
Great! You're almost halfway through!
ALMOST HALFWAY?! ARE YOU OUT OF BATTERIES?!

That's it! Keep up the pace!
PUFF! PANT!
WOOF! WOOF!
Ready to sprint?
NO! HUFF!
Go! Now!
OKAY... BUT ONLY TO REACH...
...THE BENCH! PHEW! HUFF...
Well done! Excellent rhythm!
OH, SHUT UP.

FIRST JOG OF THE SEASON, HUH?
HOW COULD YOU TELL?
THE NEW SHOES, FOR STARTERS... AND YOU LOOK BEAT.
OH...
SPRINT! NOW!
EXCUSE ME?
NOTHING! IT'S THE TRACKER... I FORGOT TO SWITCH IT OFF.
ANYWAY, IT'S NOT MY FIRST RUN OF THE SEASON... IT'S MY FIRST RUN *EVER*!
THEN YOU SHOULD WALK BEFORE YOU RUN.
WALK FIVE LAPS AROUND THE PARK EVERY DAY FOR A WEEK. THEN WE'LL TALK.

AND YOU DON'T NEED A TRACKER YET!
RIGHT!
Are you ready to—
SHUSH.
CLICK
Exercise: OKAY! But While Being Smart About It!
HEY, I'M ALMOST DONE! ALL THAT'S LEFT IS...
Study French!
And Learn to Apologize!
YEAH...

"FRENCH WON'T BE A PROBLEM. WILL'S GOING TO HELP ME, SINCE..."
...YOU JUST TOOK A LANGUAGE COURSE, YEAH?
MAIS OUI! OF COURSE!
BUT WHY DO YOU WANNA LEARN FRENCH?
I'M CURIOUS. PARIS MUST BE AN AMAZING CITY...
PLUS, FRANCE HAS SOME OF THE BEST MUSEUMS IN THE WORLD. THE FOOD IS DELICIOUS AND—
YOU WANNA READ FASHION MAGAZINES IN THEIR ORIGINAL LANGUAGE, DON'CHA?
WELL, THAT TOO.
SO? LET'S START WITH THE LESSONS.
TOMORROW! I'VE GOTTA GO SET THE TABLE FOR DINNER.

BUT I CAN GIVE YOU SOME BOOKS NOW.
YES, PLEASE.
GRAMMAR, A FEW SIMPLE NOVELS, A PHRASE BOOK FOR TOURISTS...
UM, THAT'S ENOUGH.
PARIS
NOPE. A GOOD DICTIONARY IS KEY.
OF COURSE.
FRENCH
PARIS
SEE YOU TOMORROW. AU REVOIR! BYE!
IF I DON'T FALL DOWN A MANHOLE...
FRENCH Dictionary
PARIS
SO? ARE YOU DONE WITH THE FIVE LAPS?
YES! NOW I'M ON TO WEIGHT LIFTING!
FRENCH
33

OOF! IT FEELS LIKE THIS IS MY **REGULAR** BENCH NOW.
CORNELIA!
HAY LIN! HI!
"HI"? I HAVEN'T HEARD FROM YOU IN THREE DAYS.
ER...I'VE BEEN REALLY BUSY...
I USUALLY APOLOGIZE AND THEN ***SHUT MY MOUTH.***
ACTUALLY, NO. I'M SORRY!
NO WORRIES. I'LL CALL YOU TOMORROW.
IT WORKS!

DRIIIIIIIN
CORNELIA?
I'M SORRY FOR MISSING YOUR BIRTHDAY, IRMA. AND ALSO FOR TODAY.
UH...
I WAS A BIT GROUCHY TOO...WILL YOU FORGIVE ME?
OF COURSE.
?
SEE YOU TOMORROW!
YEAH!

Learn to Apologize:
OKAY!
AWESOME! ALL DONE.
PARIS
AND IT COULD'VE GONE MUCH WORSE...
36
NGH...
FRENCH Dictionary
DLIN DLON
I'M NOT INTERESTED IN BUYING ANYTHING, BUT THANKS.
MOM, IT'S ME!
FRENCH Dictionary
OH! SO MANY BOOKS... IT'S LIKE THE *EIFFEL TOWER*.
TRUE.

HEY, SIS. ARE YOU STILL BEING WEIRD?
INDEED I AM! ISN'T IT GREAT?
PARIS
FRENCH Dictionary
LOOK, I'VE GOT A PRESENT FOR YOU.
WHAT IS IT?
A REAL FITNESS TRACKER. LISTEN...
BIP
Are you ready to sprint?
WOW! IT TALKS!
Go! Now!
YAAAY!
HEE-HEE! NOW THAT'S RUNNING.

Is she still being TOO nice?
I can't tell... Let's see.
UM...CORNELIA, CAN YOU HELP ME OUT WITH DINNER?
YES, BUT LATER! I HAVE TO SHOWER.
ALL GOOD. SHE'S BACK TO HER USUAL SELF.
I'M NOT SURE. SHE HAS A WEIRD GLINT IN HER EYES...
AND IT LOOKS LIKE SHE'S STARTED TO STUDY FRENCH.
NOW IT MAKES SENSE. TODAY WAS A DAY OF GOOD RESOLUTIONS!
YOU KNOW, ONE OF THOSE DAYS WHEN YOU DECIDE TO START EXERCISING... HUP!
...OR TO LEARN A NEW LANGUAGE. GOT IT!
SNAP

I HAVEN'T MADE ANY GOOD RESOLUTIONS IN A WHILE.
SUCH AS? BEING MORE ROMANTIC?
SUCH AS... SHALL WE DANCE?
CERTAINLY, MY PRINCE.
Excellent rhythm!
I KNOW.
YOU'RE FUNNY.
AND FINALLY...
WHAT A DAY!
39

AND I HAVEN'T LOOKED IN THE MIRROR FOR HOURS AT THIS POINT.
Be Less Obsessed with My Appearance: OKAY!
OH WELL...
GOOD NIGHT, GORGEOUS!
GOOD NIGHT, SIS!
BACK TO YOUR ROOM, LILIAN.
Ready to sprint?
END OF CHAPTER 118

YouWitch
Magical Moments to Experience Together!
Search
Susan and Dean's Wedding
VIDEO
SEARCH
Posted by:
TARANEE
Replay
Like
Great
Okay
So-So
Send to a Friend
Share
04:07 / 20:05
Susan and Dean's Wedding
AREN'T THEY BEAUTIFUL?
YEAH...
PROOT

WE'RE SHARING AN UNFORGETTABLE MOMENT...
PROOOT
HAY LIN? CAN YOU BE A BIT LESS EMOTIONAL?
I'M NOT EMOTIONAL! I MEAN, I AM...BUT I ALSO HAVE ALLERGIES!
OH, SURE! SINCE WHEN?
ADMIT IT, YA BIG SOFTY.
HMPH! WHAT, YOU'RE NOT EXCITED?
NOPE! I'M THE TOUGH ONE.
H-H-HANG ON...IT'S TIME FOR THE BOUQUET!
COME ON, SUSAN! CLOSE YOUR EYES!
HERE GOES!

WHOEVER CATCHES IT WILL GET MARRIED NEXT!
ME!
NO, ME!
UM... I DON'T WANT IT! EXCUSE ME!
WUP
WUP
WUP
WUP
OH...
!!!
THE TOUGH ONE, HUH?
...NO!

I C-CAN'T KEEP IT...I'M... I'M...ALLERGIC!
HEAR, HEAR... IT'S AN EPIDEMIC.
TOSS IT TO ME!
NO, ME!
JUST TOSS IT!
OKAY...
SNIFF!
WUP
WUP
WUP
HEY!
FRUMP
H-HELP! I DON'T WANT TO GET MARRIED YET!
GREAT, TOSS IT!

IT IS FUN, THOUGH.
AGH! CAREFUL!
WHAT'S GOING ON?
BUMP
NOW SMILE...
COME ON, SMILE!
CLING
ACK!
HEE-HEE! YOU SHOULD SEE YOURSELF.
CLIC
NOW *THAT'S* A SMILE!

MINE!
NO, MINE!
I THINK THE BUFFET'S OPEN, LAWRENCE.
INDEED. IT LOOKS DELICIOUS.
WUP
AND JUST LOOK AT THEM TUSSLING...
OH! FLOWERS ...?
WUP
THEY MUST BE MARZIPAN! TRY THEM.
MA'AM, YOU CAUGHT THE BRIDE'S BOUQUET.
BUT I'M ALREADY MARRIED TO MY LAWRENCE.
THEN TOSS IT!
ALL RIGHT.
AT LEAST TASTE IT FIRST!

WOW, WHAT A THROW!
STRAIGHT OUT OF THE PARK.
YOU HAPPY, HAY LIN?
SNIIIIIFF...
I'LL TAKE THAT AS A YES.
I...
...CAN'T...
...BELIEVE IT!

"LOOK AT THAT! SHE CAUGHT IT, AND SHE WASN'T EVEN INVITED."
"I BET SHE'S NOT EVEN IN A RELATIONSHIP."
"EH, DOESN'T MATTER. THE BOUQUET WILL BRING HER LUCK."
"SHE'LL MEET SOMEONE, AND THEN...WHO KNOWS!"
THE END

"I hear the melody of your heart."

Music in the Air

SHEFFIELD INSTITUTE—SCHOOL IS DONE FOR THE DAY.
DRIIIIN
IT'S TIME TO RUSH OUT, TIME FOR STOMACHS TO GRUMBLE, TIME FOR FREEDOM...
GROOWL
STOMK
...FOR EVERYONE... EXCEPT HAY LIN.
SHE CAN'T FREE HERSELF... FROM A CERTAIN THOUGHT.
A **NICE** THOUGHT OF A CHARMING SMILE AND TWINKLING EYES. A THOUGHT CALLED...
WES... **WESLEY HAMP!**
SHE'S THINKING... THAT SHE CAN'T STOP THINKING ABOUT HIM!
HAY-HAY! DIDN'T YOU HEAR THE BELL?
HUH? WH-WHAT BELL?
SHE'S NOW THINKING OF HOW IT ALL STARTED WITH A BELL, ABOUT TEN DAYS AGO...

DLIN DLON
THE SILVER DRAGON
CHINESE RESTAURANT
WE HAVE CUSTOMERS ALREADY?
I'LL CHECK!
3
FEBR
LUNAR NEW YEAR IS A BIG DEAL AT THE RESTAURANT, AS PER TRADITION.
AND LIKE ALWAYS, CHEN HIRED A FULL CHINESE ORCHESTRA.
ALL THE FURNITURE WAS MOVED TO MAKE SPACE FOR THE MUSICIANS...
DLIN DLON DLIN DLON
...AND TO ACCOMMODATE EXTRA RESERVATIONS FOR THE OCCASION.
COMING, COMING!
DLIN DLON
RESERVED
THERE WERE NO GUESTS YET, BUT HAY LIN WAS ALREADY STRESSED...
DLIN DLON
TRUNK TRUNK
HEY! JUST A SEC—
...OH.
UM... HELLO.

DAZZLING EYES, AN AWKWARD SMILE...
I'M WITH THE BAND.
WOOOSH
...SPORTY CLOTHES, A CASUAL LOOK—HE HAD CLEARLY MISTAKEN THE ADDRESS...
NOT GONNA LET ME IN?
W-WELL... I'M AFRAID YOU'VE GOT THE WRONG PLACE...
HAY LIN DIRECTED HIM TO THE SIDE ENTRANCE OF THE BAR NEARBY, WHERE A ROCK BAND WAS PLAYING THAT NIGHT...
CHINESE RESTAURANT
FOURTH DOOR TO THE RIGHT. THAT WAY!
AH, THANKS!
NO NEED TO ASK—HE WAS OBVIOUSLY A PART OF THAT WORLD, RIGHT?
SPLASH
SPLASH
ANYWAY, HAY LIN WAS OUT OF TIME. THE FIRST CUSTOMERS WERE ARRIVING, AND THE EVENING HAD TO BE PERFECT!
HELLO, DEAR!
HELLO, MS. SMITH!

AND SHE WANTED TO LOOK PERFECT HERSELF!
DONE! **RED**, THE COLOR OF CELEBRATION.
I GOTTA HURRY! THE PLACE IS FULL.
PAPA MUST BE SERVING APPETIZERS WHILE THE ORCHESTRA PLAYS THE FIRST PIECE.
WEIRD... THE CONCERT HASN'T STARTED.
AND I SENSE SOME **TENSION** IN THE AIR. WHAT'S GOING ON?

Hey, Yang! Where's your NEPHEW?
That's what I'd like to know. I just don't get it...
Look! Finally!
PANT, HUFF! Sorry, there was a MIS-UNDERSTANDING.
Wesley Hampstead! I expected better from you.
You won't believe it, Uncle. Some girl sent me to where a ROCK BAND was rehearsing.
They thought I was the replacement they were waiting on. It took a while to persuade—
No more excuses! The audience has been waiting long enough.
I swear that's what happened! There was a girl...
Oh! THAT girl!
ACK!

THE EVENING WAS A ROARING SUCCESS...
...TILL THE VERY END!
I-I THINK I OWE YOU AN APOLOGY.
DON'T WORRY. IT WAS KINDA FUNNY.
A TRANSVERSE FLUTE IN A ROCK BAND! COULD'VE BEEN ORIGINAL, DON'CHA THINK?
BUT AS YOU CAN SEE, I WAS COMING HERE. AND I TOTALLY DON'T REGRET COMING BACK, MY DEAR...
UM...HAY LIN!
THE DAUGHTER OF CHEN AND JOAN LIN, THE OWNERS.
AH! I'M WESLEY HAMP. SON OF ARNOLD HAMP OF HEATHERFIELD AND MEI YANG OF BEIJING, THE TRUMPETER'S SISTER.

HE'S FIRST FLUTE FOR THE ORCHESTRA...
DOES HE PLAY WELL?
I BET SHE DIDN'T EVEN LISTEN AND JUST STARED AT HIM THE WHOLE TIME.
HILAAARIOUS. HE PLAYS GREAT!
SO IT WAS LOVE AT FIRST SIGHT. YOU EXCHANGED PHONE NUMBERS AND...
OH NO, NO, NO! ACTUALLY, WE MIGHT'VE NEVER MET AGAIN IF IT WASN'T FOR VIVALDI.
VIVA... WHO??
ANTONIO VIVALDI, 18TH CENTURY ITALIAN COMPOSER, CREATOR OF THE FOUR SEASONS.
YUM! MY FAVORITE PIZZA.
IRMA! A COMPOSER IS SOMEONE WHO WRITES MUSIC.
DON'T LOOK SO SHOCKED! I'VE NEVER HEARD OF HIM.
NEITHER HAD I. BUT IT'S THANKS TO HIM THAT WESLEY AND I SAW EACH OTHER AGAIN...
"OR, WELL, THANKS TO WHAT WESLEY SAID THAT NIGHT..."
SORRY AGAIN! YOU JUST DIDN'T LOOK LIKE A CLASSICAL MUSICIAN, THAT'S ALL.
AND YOU REMIND ME OF AN ARIA BY VIVALDI.

I HAD TO FIND OUT IF IT WAS AN INSULT OR A COMPLIMENT, RIGHT?
"SO THE NEXT DAY I **HAPPENED** TO PASS BY A CD SHOP..."
YEAH, RIGHT. ADMIT IT—YOU WENT THERE **ON PURPOSE**.
HA-HA!
"OKAY, YEAH. I COULDN'T RESIST!"
UM...VIVALDI, VIVALDI...
?
!!
IT'S YOU!! WHAT A **COINCIDENCE**!
THIS IS MY FAVORITE MUSIC SHOP. YOU CAN FIND A TON OF RARE SCORES. WHAT WERE YOU LOOKING FOR?

I WAS SO EMBARRASSED. I WAS GONNA CONFESS I KNEW NOTHING ABOUT CLASSICAL MUSIC, BUT WESLEY...
THOUGH IT DOESN'T MATTER, AFTER ALL, SINCE YOU FOUND ME.
!!
Wanna listen to some LIVE music? I was about to go rehearse at the park.
THE... PARK??
YEAH! IT'S ALWAYS DESERTED THIS TIME OF YEAR. MAKES IT EASY TO FOCUS.
SO... YOU COMING?
O-OKAY...

"IT WAS ONE OF THOSE BRIGHT, LATE-WINTER DAYS WHEN YOU CAN ALREADY SMELL SPRING IN THE AIR...
"WE SAT UNDER A TREE IN THE EMPTY PARK, AND WESLEY STARTED PLAYING.
"HIS MUSIC...HIS MUSIC CARESSED THE AIR...AND THE AIR CARESSED ME..."
I'M TELLING YOU, I GOT GOOSE BUMPS!

HE PLAYED VIVALDI?
BUT, GIRLS, THE POINT ISN'T WHAT HE PLAYED, BUT HOW HE DID IT!
AND SOME MODERN PIECES TOO...
HUH? YOU MEAN...UPSIDE DOWN? STANDING ON ONE FOOT? NO HANDS?
I MEAN...HE SPOKE THROUGH THE NOTES, LIKE HE WAS ONE WITH THE MUSIC.
HEE HEE!
She's HEAD OVER HEELS, is what she means.
I'VE NEVER FELT SO... LIGHT AND HAPPY. AND WESLEY'S ALWAYS SO SWEET, ATTENTIVE AND...
WAIT—BEFORE YOU FLY OFF, LOVEBIRD... "ALWAYS"?
YOU WENT OUT AGAIN?
WELL, YEAH...A FEW TIMES.
AND...??

NOTHING! WE DID NORMAL STUFF. I WENT WITH HIM TO THE LIBRARY, HE HELPED ME CARRY MY GROCERIES HOME...
UGH, BOOORING.
SO WHEN ARE YOU TWO GONNA *KISS*?
I... UM...
I HOPE IT'LL BE ***NEXT MONDAY***.
AHAAAA! I KNEW IT! SPILL THE BEANS!
CLAP
CLAP
CLAP
WHAT'S SPECIAL ABOUT MONDAY? HUH?
'COS WES WANTS TO TAKE ME OUT TO LUNCH AFTER SCHOOL AND...
HANG ON. MONDAY'S NOT JUST ANY DAY. IT'S ***VALENTINE'S DAY***!
EXACTLY.

14 FEBRUARY
"THAT MIGHT BE THE MOMENT, RIGHT?"
OH NO. AFTER WE CAME ALL THIS WAY.
I SHOULD'VE CALLED IN ADVANCE. I'M SO SORRY, HAY LIN.
AELE
TALIAN
CUISINE
SED ON
NDAYS
MENU
THERE GOES LUNCH, I'M AFRAID. BY NOW...
UM...HOLD ON. I KNOW A PLACE...
"...WHERE WE CAN FIND SOME-THING YUMMY LAST MINUTE."
THAT WAS A GREAT IDEA! NOW WHAT?
"HOW ABOUT WE GO EAT AT THE LIGHTHOUSE?"
YUM! A PICNIC WITH A BREATHTAKING VIEW.
YEAH, THE SEA ALWAYS LOOKS SPECIAL IN WINTER...

ACTUALLY, I MEAN THIS VIEW...
!!
"OMG, HERE WE GO!
"YOU NEVER FEEL READY WHEN THE MOMENT YOU'VE BEEN WAITING FOR FINALLY COMES.
WOOOOSH
YOU OKAY, HAY LIN? YOU'RE SHIVERING.
"I'M SHAKING WITH NERVES SUDDENLY.
HERE, TAKE THIS. THE WIND'S REALLY COLD TODAY.
"I CAN CALM THE WIND AND WARM THE AIR...BUT I CAN'T CONTROL THE STORM INSIDE ME...
IF WE SNUGGLE UP, WE'LL FEEL WARMER...
"COLD SWEAT DOWN MY BACK, CHEEKS BURNING, HEART RACING...
"IF WE SNUGGLE UP, WE CAN... KISS!"

ACK!
WOOOOOSH
HUH?
DON'T WORRY! I'LL GET IT.
WES!
WOOOOOSH
STOP! WHERE'RE YOU GOING?
WOOOSH
FORGET IT, WES! WES, LOOK OUT—
SPLASH
OH NOOO!
SEE? GOT IT!
......

Golden
TUESDAY AFTERNOON, THE GOLDEN.
I SHOULD'VE STOPPED THE WIND...
PFFT! IT'S OKAY, HAY-HAY. WET LIPS CAN STILL KISS.
IRMA! THERE WAS NO KISS!
OH, SORRY. I THOUGHT THAT AFTER...
NO, WES WAS TOTALLY SOAKED, AND I FELT SO GUILTY...
CHEER UP, HAY LIN. THAT ONLY MEANS IT WASN'T THE RIGHT TIME YET.
REALLY?
OF COURSE. WATCH, IT'LL COME WHEN YOU LEAST EXPECT IT.
I KEEP THINKING IT'LL HAPPEN.
MAYBE IN THE NEXT FEW DAYS...

BUT IT DOESN'T COME ON WEDNESDAY ...
THANKS FOR WALKING ME HOME, WES.
YOU KNOW, I WISH YOU LIVED FARTHER SO WE HAD MORE TIME TO CHAT AND PLAN NEW DATES AND...
AND...?
AND THIS...
!!
SBAM
THERE YOU ARE, HAY LIN. IT TOOK YOU AGES TO COME BACK FROM SCHOOL. I WAS STARTING TO WORRY...
PLUNF
D-DON'T WORRY, MAMA. NOTHING HAPPENED...
NOT YET!

AND NOT ON FRIDAY EITHER...
AWESOME, RIGHT? I'VE SEEN IT TEN TIMES, AND I'M STILL NOT BORED.
SPACE INVADERS
-YAWN- YEAH, DEFINITELY...
I HEARD YOU SNORING THROUGH THE FIRST HALF, YANNO.
WHAT ARE YOU TALKING ABOUT?
I WAS SIMPLY USING AN ALIEN LANGUAGE TO EXPRESS MY ENTHUSIASM.
PFFFT! OKAY, OKAY. NEXT TIME, YOU PICK THE MOVIE.
BUT IT'S A SHAME YOU DON'T LIKE STORIES ABOUT UFOs...
DON'T BE MAD. I JUST PREFER ANOTHER KIND OF...
...CLOSE ENCOUNTER.

ACHOO!
?
SORRY, I, WELL...I CAUGHT A COLD THE OTHER DAY AT THE LIGHTHOUSE...
...'COS HE GAVE ME HIS JACKET, THINKING I WAS COLD!
WHAT BAD LUCK.
SO, THE AQUARIUM?
FOR WHERE TO GO ON SUNDAY, I MEAN.
OH!
THAT SOUNDS GREAT!

WILL SUNDAY BE THE DAY?
YOU KNOW WHAT I LIKE ABOUT THIS PLACE?
THE SILENCE.
WHEN IT'S RAINING, I COME HERE TO FOCUS...
I CLOSE MY EYES AND THINK...OF HOW THERE'S SO MUCH LIFE AROUND ME THAT DOESN'T MAKE ANY NOISE...
WE'RE SO USED TO USING WORDS THAT WE FORGET HOW NICE IT IS, ON OCCASION...
...TO GO WITHOUT.

HERE HE IS! I FOUND HIM, MOMMY!
HUH?
LOOK, IT'S HIM! IT'S MENO!
?
HE'S THE ONE FROM THE MOVIE. AND THAT'S HIS BROTHER, MENO MENO! SEE?
I SEE, HONEY...
HEATHERFIELD PARK, MONDAY AFTERNOON.
CHRIS IS CRAZY ABOUT THAT MOVIE TOO. I MUST'VE SEEN IT A HUNDRED TIMES...
HAY-HAY! ARE YOU LISTENING?
YOU'RE WASTING YOUR BREATH, IRMA. THE ONLY THING HAY LIN IS CRAZY ABOUT IS WESLEY.
AND IT SEEMS HE FEELS THE SAME... BUT THE BIG MOMENT OF THE FIRST KISS KEEPS GETTING DELAYED.

SHE'S ANGSTY AND BROODING BECAUSE...
...HE'S ABOUT TO LEAVE!
SWIIIS
LEAVE? WHERE TO?
HUH?
ON TOUR WITH HIS UNCLE'S ORCHESTRA.
HE PLAYED SO WELL AT NEW YEAR'S THAT THEY ASKED HIM TO JOIN...
...FOR A FEW WEEKS.
A FEW WEEKS? THAT'S AN ETERNITY...
...WHEN YOU'RE WAITING FOR THE FIRST KISS. I AGREE, IRMA!
THAT'S WHY I WISH IT WOULD HAPPEN BEFORE THEN...

BUT THE MORE YOU WANT SOMETHING, THE MORE IT SLIPS AWAY...
PHOTO BOOTH
SHOP
...ESPECIALLY WHEN PEOPLE KEEP INTERFERING!
OH, SORRY. I DIDN'T REALIZE YOU WERE THERE.
??
OR THERE'S TECH ISSUES...
ACK! MY WATCH STOPPED! WHAT'S THE TIME?
SO IN THE END, TIME'S RUNNING OUT, AND YOU STILL HAVEN'T GOT WHAT YOU HOPED FOR...
GOTTA CATCH THIS! IT'S THE ONLY TRAIN GOING MY WAY, AND I STILL HAVE TO PACK FOR TOMORROW.
...AND YOU'RE LEFT WITH ONE LAST CHANCE!
9 A.M. AT THE BUS STATION, OKAY?
I'LL BE THERE!

"I SAW YOU, UNAWARE THAT I WAS WATCHING YOU...
"...SAW YOUR EYES SUDDENLY TURN SAD...
"...SAW THE AIR FROM THE DEPARTING TRAIN RUFFLE YOUR HAIR...
74
"...AND FELT I HAD TO *CAPTURE THAT MOMENT*, THAT IMAGE, *ON PAPER*...
"...IN MY OWN WAY."

"I'LL BE THERE, WES, HAPPY AND SMILING.
CHINESE RESTAURANT
"NO LONG FACE, NO ROOM FOR SADNESS.
"WE'LL SAY GOOD-BYE, MAYBE HUG...
"...AND MAYBE THE KISS THAT KEEPS DODGING US WILL HAPPEN.
"AND IF NOT, WELL...IT'LL COME EVENTUALLY, YEAH?
"'COS THIS IS SEE YOU LATER, NOT FAREWELL!
"I'LL SET MY ALARM *TWO HOURS EARLY*...
"SO I'LL HAVE TIME TO DRESS UP AND NOT HAVE TO RUSH TO THE STATION...
"AND...WHY NOT? I'LL WRITE YOU A NOTE TOO.
"I'D DO IT NOW IF I HAD TIME, BUT...
HAY LIN!!
"...I GOTTA GO!"

SATURDAY NIGHT. FOR SOME, IT'S TIME TO GO OUT...
...AND FOR OTHERS, IT'S TIME TO COME IN!
WOULD YOU MIND GIVING US A HAND TONIGHT, HONEY?
URK! SO MANY CUSTOMERS!
TIME TO GET READY TO LEAVE...
WES! ARE YOU FINISHED PACKING?
UM... ALMOST, MOM!
...AND HANDLE THE ARRIVALS!
GOOD EVENING! DO YOU HAVE A RESERVATION?
NO, DEAR, BUT IT'S A SPECIAL OCCASION. IF THERE'S ANY CHANCE...
OF COURSE. I'LL FIND YOU A TABLE...ER... SOMEWHERE.
AND WHEN THE LIGHTS FINALLY GO OUT AND EVERYONE HEADS TO BED...
...SOME PEOPLE SLEEP MORE DEEPLY THAN OTHERS.
FLOMF

DRIIIINN
MUCH MORE DEEPLY...
...SO DEEP THEY DON'T HEAR...
...THE ALARM! HUFF...I KNEW IT! I SHOULD'VE SET TWO! OR THREE! EVERY ALARM IN THE HOUSE—
AH!
VROOOOOOM
NOOOO! WAIT! I'M HERE, WESLEY! HOLD ON!
NGH... WAIT... WAIT FOR ME...
EEEEK!!

OUCH! THAT HURTS. WHAT...?
OH, IT WAS JUST A **DREAM**. A TERRIBLE NIGHTMARE, BUT...
WHAT TIME IS IT?
AAAAAH! IT'S **SUPER-LATE**! I'LL NEVER MAKE IT TO THE BUS STATION IN TIME!
AT LEAST NOT ON PUBLIC TRANSPORT. BUT MAYBE...
SWISSs
...MAYBE I'VE GOT AN **ALTERNATIVE**, ONE THAT'S FASTER, WITH **TIRES**...

UGH! FLAT TIRES! OH NO...
FRAGILE
THERE'S GOTTA BE A SOLUTION. THINK, THINK, THINK...
GOT IT! WILL'S THE SOLUTION!
"IT'S SUNDAY MORNING. I HOPE SHE'S NOT STILL ASLEEP."
NOPE, I'VE BEEN AWAKE FOR HOURS!
Phew! Thank goodness. You're the only one who can help me.
The thing is...blah, blah...so late... blah, blah... station...
UM, YOU KNOW WHAT? I'LL BE RIGHT OVER WITH MY RATTLING RED ROCKET.
AND NOT, AS YOU ASKED, TO LEND YOU THE BIKE...

...BUT TO PERSONALLY TAKE YOU THERE!
SKREEEEK
WE'VE GOT LESS THAN HALF AN HOUR!
WE'LL MAKE IT.
HOLD ON TIGHT AND DON'T WORRY, OKAY? I'M AN EXCELLENT CYCLIST.
ACTUALLY, WILL, I WAS WONDERING...
ZOOOOW
...COULDN'T YOU, YANNO, GO A BIT FASTER? TIME IS TIGHT.
HEY, I'M GOING AS FAST AS I CAN. WANNA JOIN FORCES?
"GLADLY!"
A BIT OF MAGIC...
FFFFFF

...AND LET'S FLY LIKE THE WIIIIIND!
WHOA! THIS ISN'T...TOO MUCH, RIGHT?
CHILL, WILL. THEY'RE ALL SO BUSY DOWN THERE...
...IT'S RARE THAT ANYONE STOPS TO LOOK AT THE SKY!
WELL, IN THAT CASE...
...WE CAN GO WILD! AHHHHHHH!
WHOOOO!
WHAT...? HAY LIN?!
YOU OKAY, KID?
Y-YEAH, UNCLE. I MUST STILL BE HALF-ASLEEP...
PAT PAT
I WANTED TO SEE HER SO MUCH, I DREAMED OF HER...

"...WITH MY EYES OPEN."
OH NOOO! I WASN'T EXPECTING THIS.
YIKES! LOOKS LIKE WESLEY AND HIS ORCHESTRA AREN'T THE ONLY ONES LEAVING THIS MORNING...
HOW ARE WE GONNA FIND THE RIGHT BUS?
NO CLUE, BUT WE GOTTA HURRY. WES TOLD ME THEY'RE DEPARTING...
...AT NINE!
TLAK
VRMMMMMMMMM
SORRY...HUFF...EXCUSE ME...LET ME THROUGH— IT'S URGENT!
HEY! WATCH WHERE YOU'RE GOING!
OVER THERE! THAT BUS JUST STARTED ITS ENGINE!
WHERE? WHERE?
HAY LIN! WAIT!

VRRRMMMM
M MMM
VRRMMMMM M
WES!
VRRRMM MMMM
HAY LIN! I KNEW YOU'D COME.
?
QUICK, HOP ON! IT'S YOUR LAST CHANCE.
HUH?
VRRMMMMM
HRGH! YOU GOOD?
"YES, WILL. AND NOW I'M SURE... THE *RIGHT MOMENT HAS COME*!
"AND LIKE ALL THE BEST THINGS, *IT WASN'T ANYTHING LIKE I IMAGINED...*"
VRRMMMM
VRRMMMM

...BUT IT WAS BEAUTIFUL.
UM... CAN YOU GET DOWN NOW?
"I WANNA JUMP OFF, RUN TO YOUR SIDE, AND NEVER LEAVE YOU AGAIN, HAY LIN...
"BUT I GOTTA GO...
"AND YOUR KISS WILL KEEP ME COMPANY DURING THIS LONG TRIP...
"YOU KNOW, I ALSO HAVE SOMETHING FOR YOU WHILE WE'RE APART..."
HAY LIN, RIGHT? I'M MAGGIE.
DO I...KNOW YOU?
MY BROTHER WESLEY WAS SURE YOU'D COME...AND NOW I GET WHY.
HE ASKED ME TO GIVE YOU THIS IN CASE HE COULDN'T DO IT IN PERSON...
OH... THANKS!

"DEAR HAY LIN, I'M SORRY THESE LAST FEW DAYS WERE SO FRANTIC...
Dear Hay Lin
"MAYBE YOU'RE FEELING A BIT SAD NOW...
"...AND YOU'RE WONDERING IF WHAT BLOSSOMED BETWEEN US IS BOUND TO BE OVER NOW THAT I'M LEAVING...
"...OR IF WE'LL MEET AGAIN WHEN I COME BACK...
"THE ANSWER IS INSIDE THIS ENVELOPE.
For Hay
"*MUSIC IN THE AIR*" — DEDICATED TO *HAY LIN*...
"I WROTE IT WHILE THINKING ABOUT YOU..."

HEY, HONEY. DID YOU HAVE FUN WITH WILL?
"YOU'RE HOLDING THE ORIGINAL, THE ONLY COPY THAT EXISTS...
"I ENTRUST IT TO YOU... ALONG WITH MY HEART. KEEP BOTH SAFE TILL I COME BACK...
YOU CAME BACK EARLY. IS EVERYTHING OKAY?
"ONLY THEN, ONCE WE'RE TOGETHER AGAIN, WILL I BE ABLE TO PLAY IT—
?
"OUR MUSIC... AND I HOPE IT'LL LAST FOREVER.
"XOXO, WESLEY."
END OF CHAPTER 119

YouWitch
Magical Moments to Experience Together!
Search
Kitchen Catastrophes
VIDEO
SEARCH
Posted by:
WILL
Replay
Like
Great
Okay
So-So
Send to a Friend
Share
"MIX THE BATTER IN A BOWL..."
WILL...IT DOESN'T SAY TO USE A WHISK.
TRUST ME. IT'LL BE FASTER.
VRRR
PERFECT! WHAT NEXT?
YOU HAVE EYES, RIGHT?
04:07 / 20:05 Kitchen Catastrophes
DON'T MAKE FUN OF ME.
OKAY, BUT TRY FOLLOWING THE RECIPE.
WHY? I WANNA BE FREE!
OUCH! MY FINGER!
TUMP

YOU GOTTA BE CREATIVE IN THE KITCHEN! C'MON, LET'S ADD SOME RANDOM STUFF!
HAAH...
IT'LL BE MORE EXCITING IF I PICK THE INGREDIENTS WITH MY EYES CLOSED.
YEAH, I'M ALREADY TREMBLING.
HERE! I'M SURE THIS WILL GIVE IT A UNIQUE FLAVOR.
OH, SURE— OF DISH SOAP!
ER...BETTER OPEN MY EYES. BUT LOOK—
THE PERFUME YOU GOT ME FOR CHRISTMAS. WHAT'S IT DOING HERE?
I DON'T WANNA KNOW. C'MON, LET'S FOLLOW THE RECIPE!
HOW BORING. I'LL HAVE YOU KNOW, MY FRIENDS ARE MUCH WORSE THAN ME IN THE KITCHEN. ESPECIALLY TARANEE.
GREAT! DON'T INVITE ME IF YOU HAVE A DINNER PARTY.
Cooking

TARA, THIS IS YOUR GREAT-GREAT-GRANDMA **GRACE**'S RECIPE BOOK.
ERGH! DOES IT EXPLAIN HOW TO GET **KETCHUP** OUT OF THE BOTTLE?
THIS ISN'T A JOKE. IT'S A VERY PRECIOUS ANTIQUE, AND I'M ENTRUSTING IT TO YOU.
YEAH?
THESE RECIPES WERE PASSED DOWN FROM GENERATION TO GENERATION...
AGH!
SBLOT
...CAREFULLY WRITTEN DOWN BY OUR ANCESTORS. BUT THE MOST IMPORTANT THING...
UGH, IT'S NOT COMING OFF!
...IS THAT WHOEVER OWNS THE BOOK MUST LEAVE THEIR **MARK** ON IT.
AND SINCE IT'S A RECIPE BOOK, THAT MEANS IT HAS TO BE A **FOOD STAIN**!
OH!

YOUR GREAT-GREAT-GRAN STAINED IT WITH OIL, HER DAUGHTER WITH WHIPPED CREAM...
...AND EVENTUALLY, IT GOT TO ME, AND I STAINED IT WITH COFFEE.
NOW IT'S YOUR TURN.
UM... DONE! WITH *KETCHUP!*
BUT...BUT...YOU HAVEN'T COOKED ANYTHING YET.
I'M ALWAYS ONE STEP AHEAD! I TAKE AFTER YOU.
I DON'T KNOW IF I SHOULD HUG YOU OR YELL AT YOU...
THE FIRST ONE!
DON'T COMPLAIN! IF YOU KNEW WHAT CORNELIA DID...

WHATCHA DOING, SIS?
INVENTING THE MOST DISGUSTING RECIPE IN HISTORY. THERE'S A PRIZE!
I'M CHECKING ON YOUCHEF TO SEE IF ANYONE'S ALREADY MADE SOMETHING SIMILAR...
CHILI PEPPERS, CAKE MIX, OLIVES, STRAWBERRY MERINGUE...
...PINEAPPLE, HOT DOG, APRICOT JAM, ANCHOVIES...OH NO!
YOUCHEF
A SIMILAR RECIPE WAS POSTED BY SOME GUY CALLED BOB.
YUM...
A SMOOTHIE! CAN I HAVE A TASTE?
NO! DON'T—
...DAD!
CORNY? IRMA TEXTED YOU. SHE SAYS TO CALL HER BACK...

I THINK YOU USED TOO MUCH YEAST, IRMA...
DUM-DUM-DUM... WHAT?
TOO MUCH YEAST!
NAH, I FOLLOWED THE DIRECTIONS... MOM, YOU SHOULD REALLY LISTEN TO THIS.
AND YOU SHOULD TURN THAT THING OFF! WHEN YOU'RE COOKING, YOU HAVE TO CONCENTRATE.
POMEGRANATE? NO, I PREFER APPLES...
I'M SERIOUS! YOU USED TOO MUCH...
?
POP
...YEAST.
WOW! WHAT AN EXPLOSIVE OUTRO. MOM, YOU GOTTA LISTEN TO THIS!
BREEEP
BREEEP
BREEEP

YOU'RE COOKING? ME TOO!
HAROLD, CAN YOU STOP BRUSHING YOUR TEETH AND TELL ME WHAT HAPPENED?
HMM... NOT THAT BAD...
"COOKING" ISN'T QUITE THE RIGHT WORD.
ALL THIS TALK OF FOOD IS MAKING ME HUNGRY.
I KNOW! LET'S GO TO HAY LIN'S RESTAURANT AND STUFF OURSELVES WITH SPRING ROLLS.
CAN'T! I'VE GOT A SITUATION HERE! SEE YOU AT THE PIZZA PLACE!
HAY LIN! I ASKED YOU TO TURN THE FLAME OFF TEN MINUTES AGO!
93

SO...
YOU KNOW, YOU CAN TELL A LOT ABOUT PEOPLE FROM THE WAY THEY EAT PIZZA.
PIZZA
MENU
I...⇝MUNCH⇜... FOLD IT! WHAT DOES THAT MEAN?
THAT YOU'RE IN A HURRY TO EAT. YOU'RE THE HUNGRY TYPE.
I CUT IT IN SLICES.
THE ORDERLY TYPE.
I START FROM THE MIDDLE.
GLUTTON TYPE. AND WILL AND MATT ARE... THE LOVEBIRD TYPE.
WHY? ⇝NOM⇜...HOW CAN YOU TELL?
OH, NOTHING... JUST A HUNCH.
Cornelia, though, is the DISTRACTED type.
Give me a bite!
THE END

120

"The energy of life is life itself."
Lady Giga

HEATHERFIELD, WILL'S ROOM, 3 A.M.
UM...UGH...C'MON! WHERE ON EARTH ARE YOU TAKING ME...
...NASH?
TRUST ME— YOU'LL LIKE IT!

I'M OBVIOUSLY DREAMING...
...AND THAT'S WHY I DON'T THINK I SHOULD BE HERE **WITH YOU**!
IF IT'S JUST SOME DREAM, WHAT ARE YOU SO WORRIED ABOUT?
ARE YOU AFRAID **MATT** WILL SEE US TOGETHER?
'COURSE NOT! WHY WOULD I BE? THIS IS A DREAM, AFTER ALL.
AHEM! WHAT AM I SAYING?
YOU CAN'T LIE IN DREAMS. WILL, YOU **WARM** MY HEART.

WARM TO THE POINT...
...OF...
...MELTING!
WELL, WELL, WELL...
LOOK WHO FELL...
...INTO OUR TRAP!

AH!
WH-WHAT A NIGHTMARE! NOT ONLY DO I HAVE A SORE THROAT, I GUESS I'M DELIRIOUS TOO...
...HUH?
FRRRZZZZZ

WHAT...?
ACK!
THIS KIND OF ENERGY CAGE IS BOTH REAL...
FZZZZZ
...AND ALIVE!
SLASH
WHOA!

SLAAASH
IT'S TRYING TO CAPTURE ME!
WAIT—
IT'S COMING OUT OF THE ELECTRIC SOCKET.
MAYBE IF I CAN GET TO...
...THE CIRCUIT BREAKER ...!

SLAAASHH
NGH!
CLUNCK
RRRSSHHH
OOF! JUST IN TIME. THANK GOODNESS I WAS WEARING MY SCARF.
FINGERS CROSSED I DIDN'T WAKE MY WHOLE FAMILY UP WITH THAT RUCKUS.

NOPE, THANK GOODNESS! SLEEPING LIKE BABIES.
NOW TO FIGURE OUT WHAT'S GOING ON. THAT HAD TO BE A **MAGICAL** ATTACK...
...FUELED BY **ELECTRICITY** SOMEHOW.
I SHOULD **TRANSFORM** AND GO TELL THE GIRLS.
OKAY, SOUNDS LIKE A PLAN. I'LL CONTACT THEM **TELEPATHICALLY** ALONG THE WAY...

"...SO I DON'T SCARE THEM OUT OF BED."
OH NO!
NO WONDER CORNELIA DIDN'T ANSWER MY TELEPATHIC MESSAGES. THESE MARKS ON HER BEDROOM FLOOR...
...SHE WAS SURROUNDED BY THAT ELECTRIC CAGE TOO.
SO SHE'S BEEN CAUGHT... BUT BY WHO? AND WHY?
I JUST HOPE THE OTHERS DIDN'T FALL INTO THE SAME TRAP!

BUT...
THIS IS A NIGHTMARE! MAYBE I'M STILL SLEEPING...
TARANEE AND HAY LIN ARE ALSO GONE. THAT ONLY LEAVES IRMA...
...BUT I'M NOT OPTIMISTIC, SINCE SHE'S NOT RESPONDING EITHER...
?
ROOONF
106

IRMA! IRMA, WAKE UP!
MMM...WHO IS IT? THE TOOTH FAIRY?
NO! IT'S WILL! WHY DIDN'T YOU ANSWER MY TELEPATHIC CALL?
HUH?
I THOUGHT I HEARD A BUZZING! SO IT WAS YOU, NOT A HOARSE MOSQUITO.
HOARSE ?
IT'S 'COS OF YOUR SORE THROAT. YOUR THOUGHTS ARE AFFECTED TOO. YOU SHOULD DRINK SOME MILK WITH HONEY.
I'M NOT HERE TO GET HEALTH ADVICE! AND I'M NOT DRESSED LIKE THIS TO GET YOUR TEETH! YOU GONNA WAKE UP OR WHAT?
EEP!

SHORTLY AFTER...
WILL YOU QUIT IT?
YOU MIGHT BE HOARSE, BUT YOU SURE ARE LOUD!
THAT DREAM THING IS WEIRD...WHY D'YA THINK IT WAS ABOUT NASHTER?
HE'S MAGICAL, LIKE US. AND IF I'M NOT MISTAKEN, HE'S STILL IN HEATHERFIELD.
YOU THINK HE KNOWS SOMETHING ABOUT WHY OUR FRIENDS DISAPPEARED?
NO, BUT I BELIEVE YOU DREAMED ABOUT HIM FOR A REASON.
COULD IT BE THAT DEEP DOWN YOU HAVE A CRUSH ON THE BLOND ALIEN GUY? HMM?
OH, C'MON!

INSTEAD OF BEING SILLY, EXPLAIN WHY YOU WEREN'T CAPTURED LIKE THE OTHERS.
UM...YOU SAID THE KIDNAPPER USES ELECTRICITY, RIGHT? BUT LAST NIGHT, WE LOST POWER TO THE HOUSE!
"DAD BLAMED ME, MOM, AND CHRISTOPHER. HE THINKS WE TURNED ON ALL THE HOME APPLIANCES AT THE SAME TIME."
URRRRUUUU
TWING
BING
ZAP
BUT IS IT MY FAULT I NEED TO TURN UP THE RADIO WHEN I USE THE HAIR DRYER?
SO YOU CAUSED A LUCKY BLACKOUT.
I WOULDN'T SAY LUCKY. I WENT TO BED WITH WET HAIR!

ACHOOO!
THERE, SEE? NOW I'M GONNA GET A SORE THROAT TOO.
THE FACT OF THE MATTER IS, I SHOULDN'T BE FLYING AROUND AT THIS TIME OF NIGHT.
OUR FRIENDS ARE IN DANGER, AND ALL YOU CAN DO IS COMPLAIN?
LOOK WHO'S TALKING. ALL YOU CAN DO IS ADMIRE YOUR REFLECTION.
?
I'M NOT! THE CAMERAS OF THIS ELECTRONICS SHOP ARE RECORDING ME!

BUT... WHAT...?
AND THE BANK'S SECURITY CAMERA ON THE OTHER SIDE OF THE STREET...
WHO'S WATCHING US?
SOMEONE WHO CAN CONTROL THE CITY'S POWER GRID.
LOOK! THE TRAFFIC LIGHTS!
EVEN THE SHOP SIGNS ARE LIGHTING UP AND...
...LEADING US IN A SPECIFIC DIRECTION!

SO...
I GUESS WE'VE RUN OUTTA TRAFFIC LIGHTS AT THIS POINT.
AND NO MORE STREETLIGHTS EITHER.
DE-DLENG DE DLENG
WHOA! EVEN THE RAILROAD CROSSINGS ARE OPENING THEMSELVES.
I HOPE THERE'S NO GHOST TRAIN. OR MAYBE IT JUST LEFT...
FORGIVE THE AWFUL PUN, BUT SOMETHING TELLS ME...
...WE GOTTA GO RIGHT!
OH...

THE *HYDROPOWER PLANT!* I WENT HERE ON A TRIP BACK IN ELEMENTARY SCHOOL. BUT I'VE NEVER SEEN IT LIT UP DURING THE DAY.
I FEEL LIKE I'M A MOTH BEING DRAWN TO LIGHT RIGHT NOW.
YOU THINK IT'S A TRAP?
COULD BE...BUT WE GOTTA FIND THE OTHERS AND FIGURE OUT WHAT'S GOING ON.
THAT MOUNTAIN BACK THERE...IT LOOKS LIKE THE ONE WHERE NASH TOOK ME IN MY DREAM!

AH, DREAMS! PEOPLE READ TOO MUCH INTO THEM, YOU KNOW?
?
BUT THE SIMPLE TRUTH IS...
...THEY'RE JUST THE PRODUCT OF ELECTRICAL ACTIVITY! A MERE EXCHANGE OF SPARKS BETWEEN THE NEURONS IN YOUR BRAIN.
CORNELIA! HAY LIN!
TARANEE!

WE'RE A BIT SINGED, BUT WE'RE FINE. DON'T COME ANY CLOSER!
YEAH! I DUNNO HOW, BUT THIS LADY WITH THE **'80s PERMED HAIR** MANAGED TO GET THE DROP ON US.
AND SHE ALSO **MAGNETIZED US** SO WE'RE STUCK TO THE TURBINES.
WHO ARE YOU? WHAT DO YOU WANT FROM US?
IF YOU REALLY NEED A NAME, YOU CAN CALL ME ***LADY GIGA***.
IT'S EASY TO MOVE BETWEEN THE INFINITE ELECTRICAL NETWORK OF A TECHNOLOGICAL WORLD ***RIPE*** WITH ENERGY!
AS FOR YOU, I'VE BEEN ***STUDYING*** YOU FOR A WHILE, HIDING IN YOUR COMPUTERS, BETWEEN THE SIGNALS OF YOUR CELL PHONES...

WE'VE DEFEATED MUCH TOUGHER ENEMIES THAN YOU! WHERE'D YOU COME FROM?
THAT DOESN'T CONCERN YOU, GIRL...
SLASH
SHATRZZZ
YOU SHOULD WORRY ABOUT WHERE I WANT TO GO!
VRRRATTZZ
NNNGH!
AAAH!
I FEED OFF ALL KINDS OF ENERGY, LIKE A VAMPIRE. AND HEATHERFIELD'S FULL OF THE BEST TYPE— MAGICAL ENERGY!
AND THAT'S THANKS TO YOU. SO I NEED YOUR ENERGY TO AWAKEN MY SISTERS!
VRAAAAATZZZ

I-I CAN'T...
VRAAAAAATRZZ
RESISTANCE IS FUTILE! IN HERE, YOUR STRENGTH...
VRRRRTZZZ
...IS MINE!
AAAAH!
SBAM
YES! THE WHOLE PLANET IS BRIMMING WITH ENERGY! THE ONLY ISSUE...
...IS THAT IT'S ALSO FULL OF LIVING BEINGS!
SHAATRZ

SHARTRZZ
THERE'S WAY TOO MANY FOR MY TASTE.
SEEMS LIKE... SHE CAN'T STAND **CONTACT** WITH OTHER THINGS.
SHE'S SUSPENDED IN SOME SORTA **ENERGY FIELD** THAT SHIELDS HER FROM THE OUTSIDE WORLD.
BUT NOT ALL OF EARTH'S CREATURES ARE USELESS. YOU, FOR EXAMPLE...
...POSSESS SOMETHING TRULY **PRECIOUS**!
?
WHIIINN

AH! WHAT THE—
FUZZZ
DON'T FIGHT IT! LET MY SWEET ELECTRO-PROBES POKE AROUND YOUR PRETTY LITTLE HEADS.
THAT'S IT! AS I SAID, THE HUMAN BRAIN HAS ITS OWN ELECTRICITY.
THE NEURONS POSSESS POSITIVE AND NEGATIVE CHARGES...
...THAT CAN BE TRANSFORMED, SIPHONED OFF...
FRAAATZZZ
...AND CHANNELED IN A SPECIFIC DIRECTION.
WAAAM
CRASH

SBAAAM
CRASH
KRAAAMMMM
HA-HA-HA! YES! MARVELOUS! WHAT POWER! PURE MAGICAL ENERGY!
WOOOSHHH
IT'S FUTILE TO RESIST. CLOSE YOUR EYES, RELAX, AND LISTEN TO THE SOUND OF MY VOICE.
LET YOUR REASON VANISH, YOUR MIND SHUT DOWN... CELL BY CELL... NEURON BY NEURON...

ITS ICY CLOAK SHIMMERS. ITS METAL HEART BEATS...
"IT RINGS OUT IN THE NIGHT A SONG GLOOMY AND BLEAK...
"...AND RUNS LIKE THE WIND ATOP ITS STEED..."
ITS ICY CLOAK SHIMMERS...
HOW...HOW AWFUL! SHE STARTED TO SING!
I THINK IT'S A LULLABY TO SEND US TO SLEEP—PERMANENTLY! DON'T LISTEN TO HER, IRMA. CAN YOU HEAR MY THOUGHTS?
I-I CAN, WILL! YOU DIDN'T DRINK ANY HONEY YET, DID YOU?

GOOD! KEEP SAYING SILLY STUFF. AS LONG AS WE CAN THINK, WE CAN REACT.
WE'RE SUPER-CLOSE TO WATER! WATER, YOU GET IT? CAN YOU ABSORB ITS POWER?
H-HONESTLY, NOT REALLY.
THAT STUPID SONG'S LIKE A HAMMER IN MY HEAD!
DON'T FALL ASLEEP, IRMA. REMEMBER WHAT YOU DID WITH THE HAIR DRYER?
I...THINK I GET IT. YOU WANT ME TO SHORT-CIRCUIT THE PLANT.
EXACTLY.
I'LL TRY, BUT I CAN'T PROMISE ANYTHING.
...RINGS OUT IN THE NIGHT A SONG GLOOMY AND BLEAK...

SO WHILE LADY GIGA KEEPS SINGING AND THE MAGICAL RAY PIERCES THROUGH THE MOUNTAIN...
BLUB
BLUB
BLUB
..IRMA CALLS ON HER ELEMENT, **WATER**...
FLISH
SHAFT
...MAKING IT SEEP INSIDE THE HYDROPOWER PLANT...
FRRUUUSHH
FRUUUSHHH
...AND LETTING IT SILENTLY FLOOD THE ENGINE ROOM!

FRRZZZZZ
FRZZZ
BAM
SLASH
WHAT...?
AH!
SLASH SHATZZZ
SBRANG
KEEP IT UP, IRMA! YOU'RE WEAKENING HER ELECTRIC BARRIER. LET IN AS MUCH WATER AS YOU CAN.

FROOUUSSSH
CRASH
IT CAN'T BE! MY BARRIER'S GROWING THINNER...THE MAGICAL RAY IS VANISHING!
YOU!
THERE! A LITTLE CLOSER...
YOU'RE STILL CONSCIOUS AND STEALING ENERGY FROM MY ELECTRO-PROBES! HOW CAN YOU...?
NGH ...
GOTCHA!
?

¡¡¡SSSHHH
N-NO!
¡¡¡SSSHHH
LET ME GO! AAAH! DON'T TOUCH ME!
¡¡¡SSSHHH
PAF
HUH?
YES!

IIIISSSHHH
AAAH! STOP! YOU DON'T KNOW WHAT YOU'RE DOING! RELEASE ME!
NO WAY! YOU'RE NOT GOING...
...ANY-WHERE!
IIISSSHHHH
AAAARGH!
IISSSHHH
SPLASH

C-CURSE YOU! THIS ISN'T...
...OVER—
WOOOOOSHH
FRUUUSHH
FRZZZ
128

YOU WERE AMAZING, IRMA!
I SWEAR, I THOUGHT I WOULDN'T MAKE IT.
WHEN WE TOUCHED HER, SHE ALMOST... ***BURNED TO A CRISP.*** HOW DID YOU KNOW THAT WOULD HAPPEN?
I DIDN'T.
I HAPPENED TO NOTICE THERE WAS A BARRIER PROTECTING HER FROM OTHER LIVING BEINGS, SO I GAVE IT A SHOT.
SOMETHING TELLS ME SHE WON'T BE BACK!
ESPECIALLY NOW THAT WE KNOW HER WEAK SPOT.
I'M WORRIED ABOUT THOSE ***SISTERS*** SHE MENTIONED. LET'S HOPE SHE DIDN'T MANAGE TO ***WAKE THEM UP.***

HEATHERFIELD, WILL'S BEDROOM. 7:30 A.M...
WAKE UP, SLEEPY-HEAD!
HUH? WHAT?
WHY WERE YOU SLEEPING ON THE FLOOR?
I WASN'T SLEEPING. I WAS COMATOSE. IT'S DIFFERENT.
I DON'T QUITE UNDERSTAND, BUT OKAY. LOOK, YOU LEFT YOUR PHONE ON AND...
G-GIVE IT TO ME!
THERE!
BIIIP
YOU'RE TURNING IT OFF IN THE MORNING? WHAT'S THE MATTER?
I SURE AM! DON'CHA KNOW WE'RE SURROUNDED BY ELECTRO-MAGNETIC FIELDS?

CELL PHONES, TVs, COMPUTERS... WE SHOULD SWITCH THEM OFF SOMETIMES AND LEARN HOW TO REALLY COMMUNICATE.
MMM...MIGHT BE A COINCIDENCE, BUT SOMETHING LIKE THAT ACTUALLY HAPPENED LAST NIGHT.
OH YEAH?
YEAH. SOMEONE FLIPPED THE CIRCUIT BREAKER, AND EVERYTHING IN THE FREEZER THAWED.
OOPS!
BY THE WAY, CAN YOU TURN ON THE ELECTRIC HEATER? IT'S A BIT CHILLY.
WHICH WOULD YOU LIKE FOR BREAKFAST? STRAWBERRY OR PISTACHIO?
THANKS, DEAN. I'LL HAVE SOME TOAST.

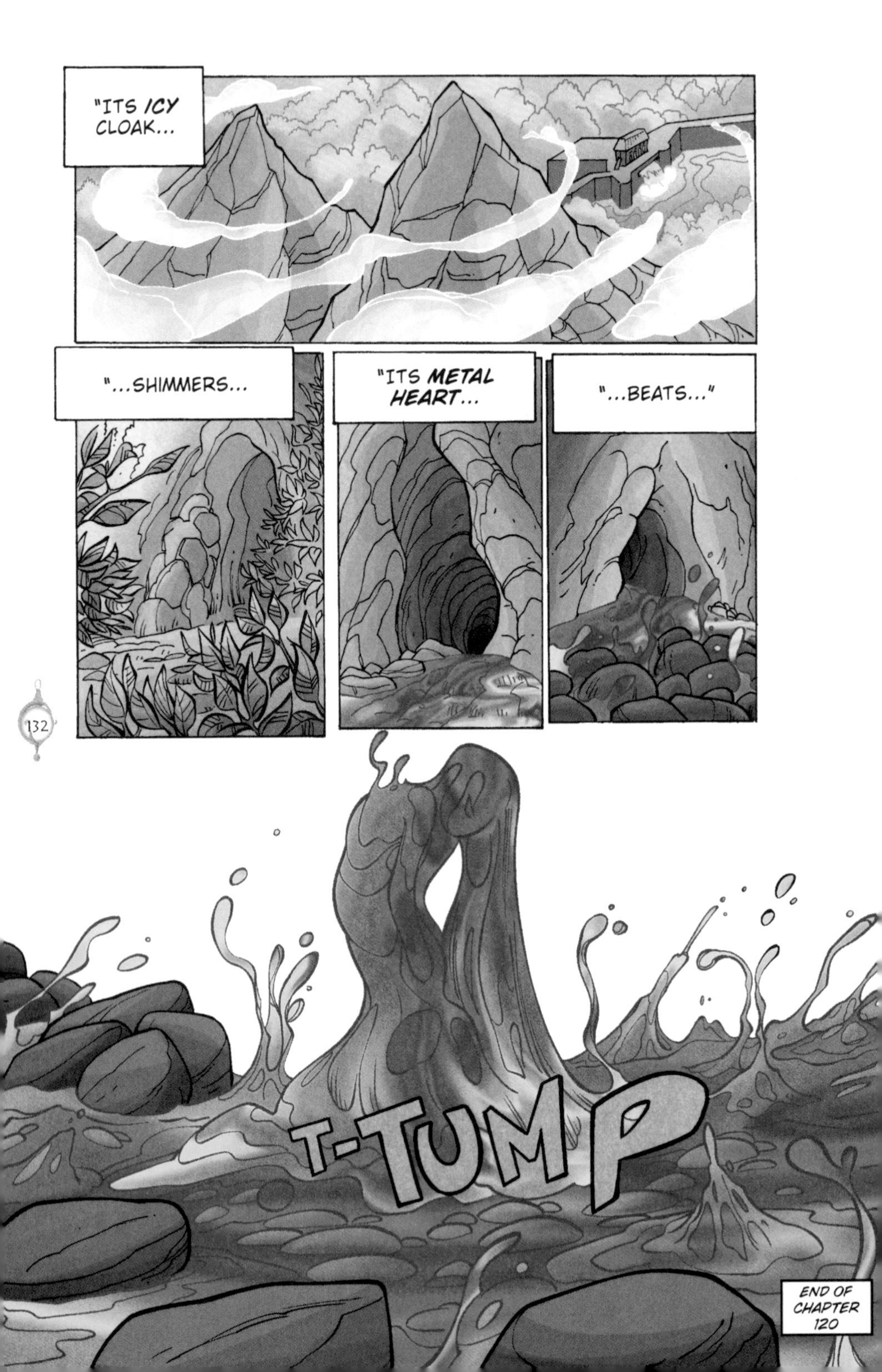
"ITS ICY CLOAK...
"...SHIMMERS...
"ITS METAL HEART...
"...BEATS..."
T-TUMP
END OF CHAPTER 120

YouWitch
Magical Moments to Experience Together!
Search
An Owl at the Window
VIDEO
SEARCH
Posted by:
CORNELIA
Replay
Like
Great
Okay
So-So
Send to a Friend
Share
LITTLE SISTER
LEAVE IT... MMM...IT'S MINE! MEANIE...
...MEAN... SNORE...
04:07 / 20:05 An Owl at the Window
I SAID THAT CRAYON'S MINE! GIVE IT TO ME!
UNBELIEVABLE. SHE'S ARGUING WITH HER CLASSMATES EVEN IN HER SLEEP.
MINE! MINE! MINE!
Shhh. Here you go.
HOO! HOO! HOO!

THANKS... MMM...
WELL, I EXPECTED WORSE...
SNORE...GIMME MY ICE CREAM! NOW!
SERIOUSLY? THIS IS CRAZY.
IT'S MINE, MINE, MINE!
A LOLLIPOP MIGHT WORK...
MMM... YUM...
THAT'S ENOUGH! DREAM ABOUT SOMETHING ELSE.
SNORE! THE ORANGE JUICE IS MINE! GIVE IT BACK!
AAAH! STOP IT!
MOM, IS THERE ANY ORANGE JUICE IN THE FRIDGE?
MMM...WHY AREN'T YOU TWO SLEEPING?
'COS IT'S FUN TO PRANK MY BIG SIS, MOM.
HOO! HOO! HOO!

LITTLE BROTHER
KISS MOMMY...
...AND DADDY!
GOOD NIGHT...
Kisses are nice, right?
Yeah!
They did that to me too when I was little.
I'll let you in on a secret...I kinda miss it.
HEY! NO FAIR!
KISSES NICE!
Hoo! Hoo! Hoo!

LITTLE BROTHER
IRMA?
HUH?
CAN I SLEEP HERE?
NO WAY.
BUT I HAD A BAD DREAM...
A HAIRY MONSTER CAME INTO MY ROOM THROUGH THE WINDOW...
...AND CRAWLED SLOWLY TO MY BED, SCRATCHING THE FLOOR WITH ITS CLAWS!
ITS BREATHING GOT CLOSER AND CLOSER...
OH NO...
Hoo! Hoo! Hoo!

AND SUDDENLY A HUGE SHADOW—
OKAY! THAT'S ENOUGH!
CAN I SLEEP HERE?
NO!
WH- WHY NOT?
'COS I'VE GOT A BETTER IDEA.
UM...CAN WE SLEEP HERE?
?
HOO! HOO! HOO!

BIG BROTHER
PETER...
MM-HMM?
LET ME GUESS— YOU HAD PIZZA WITH YOUR FRIENDS.
HOW DID YOU KNOW?
HOW DO YOU THINK? YOUR BREATH! YOU HAD GARLIC AND PEPPER PIZZA AGAIN!
I DIDN'T. I SWEAR.
IT WAS GARLIC, PEPPERS, AND ONION.
YUCK! GROSS.
DON'T KNOCK IT TILL YOU'VE TRIED IT...I BROUGHT ONE FOR YOU.
OH! REALLY?
PIZZA
COME ON! IT'S GREAT.
BUT I BRUSHED MY TEETH...
GIVE IT A TASTE.
HOO! HOO! HOO!

YUM...SO GOOD...
SEE?
IS THERE NOTHING TO DRINK?
AS IF I DON'T KNOW YOU...ORANGE SODA!
WHY ARE YOU TWO STILL UP?
MIDNIGHT SNACK, MOM.
PIZZA! WHAT KIND?
FIND OUT YOURSELF.
MMM...SO GOOD!
HEE-HEE! THAT'S WHAT I SAID.
YAWN...WHY AM I ALWAYS THE LAST TO KNOW ABOUT THINGS?
LEAVE A SLICE FOR DAD!
Hoo! Hoo! Hoo!

OWL!
I KNOW IT'S LATE...BUT I COULDN'T SLEEP.
WHAT? YOU TOO? GOOD...I CALLED THE RIGHT FRIEND, THEN.
THING IS, THERE'S AN OWL HERE WHO JUST WON'T SHUT UP...
HOO! HOO! HOO!
OH, I'LL TRADE YOU IN A HEARTBEAT.
THE HOT DOG'S MINE! MINE! MINE!
THE END

121

"The future is in your hands!"
Ten Years Later

KANDRAKAR, KINGDOM OF WISDOM AND HARMONY.
When's the ceremony gonna be over, Grandma?
Patience! It's almost time for your PRESENT.
AND NOW, LET US THANK OUR GUARDIANS...
YOU'VE BATTLED CEASELESSLY FOR MANY YEARS, SERVING THE CAUSE OF SERENITY AND LIGHT.
NOT ONCE DID YOU FAIL TO MEET KANDRAKAR'S EXPECTATIONS. O YOUNG STARS OF OUR FIRMAMENT! O UNPARALLELED GUARDIANS OF PEACE!
ZZZZ

THE ODE TO YOUR VICTORIES WILL NEVER FADE. NOR THE ECHO OF YOUR INCREDIBLE FEATS...
I think I hear something else.
RPPP
It's Irma's snoring! If I move, she'll FALL...
SNOOORE...
GRANDMA!
All right, let's go. But be quiet!
HOW CAN WE EVER REPAY YOUR NOBLE SERVICES?
What about Irma?
Wake her up gently...
HOW CAN WE EVER...
Irma... Irma?
HUH? IS IT SNACK TIME?
...REWARD THOSE WHO WATCH OVER US?

A WHILE LATER...
SNACK TIME? DON'T YOU EVER DREAM ABOUT, LIKE... PRINCE CHARMING?
I DID!
I DREAMED THAT A CUTE BLOND GUY RODE IN ON A WHITE HORSE...
AND?
HE TOOK ME TO A SUNLIT FOREST CLEARING...
AND?
AND WE HAD A PICNIC!
YOU'RE RIDICULOUS.
BUT FIRST, THE PRESENT.
PRESENT! PRESENT!
RELAX, IRMA. THEY'RE ABOUT TO SERVE REFRESH-MENTS.
WOW! WHAT A PLACE.

ALLOW ME TO INTRODUCE YOUR FUTURE. EACH DOOR OPENS TO A DAY THAT IS YET TO COME.
YOU MEAN BEHIND HERE WE CAN SEE WHAT'LL HAPPEN TO US?
PRECISELY. YOUR REWARD IS BEING ABLE TO TAKE A PEEK.
HAVEN'T WE VISITED THE FUTURE ALREADY?
YEAH, BUT WE ONLY SAW WHAT WOULD OCCUR IF WE GAVE UP MAGIC.
THIS IS DIFFERENT. THIS IS...WHAT WILL BE!
IN THEORY. BUT I WILL EXPLAIN EVERYTHING LATER...

YOU CAN ONLY OPEN A SINGLE DOOR— THE ONE THAT WILL SHOW YOU YOUR LIFE IN TEN YEARS.
HERE ARE THE KEYS. GO ON—TAKE A LOOK! I'LL BRING YOU BACK WHEN THE TIME COMES.
SEARCH THROUGH THE DOORS. THE CORRECT ONE WILL LIGHT UP.
I'VE NEVER FELT SO CURIOUS!
REALLY ?
THIS WHOLE THING STRESSES ME OUT.
WHY? AFRAID FUTURE YOU IS GONNA HAVE SPLIT ENDS?
VERY FUNNY. HERE THEY ARE... DON'T TELL ME YOU'RE NOT FREAKING OUT!
W-WELL...

WHO'S UP FIRST?
DON'T LOOK AT ME!
OF COURSE I AM.
CLAC
CLAC
TARA! YOU GOING IN?
FULL SPEED...
...AHEAD?!
TALK ABOUT FULL SPEED—I'M IN A RACE!
56

AND WHAT A RACE AT THAT. IT'S THE OLYMPICS!
CLAP
TARANEE COOK SEEMS PRETTY DISTRACTED TODAY.
CLAP
CLAP
YES, MARVIN! I WONDER WHAT'S ON HER MIND?
LOOK! MOM AND DAD ARE IN THE AUDIENCE!
WHAT'S THE MATTER? RUN!

I'M RUNNING, I'M RUNNING! HEY...
...THAT'S ME! I'M SO FIT!
WOW, I LOVE THIS FUTURE!
DAAARLING!
DAAARLING! RUN LIKE I'M WAITING FOR YOU AT THE FINISH LINE!
HUH?
THAT'S MY BOYFRIEND?
YOO-HOOO!
RUN! RUN! RUN!
AND OVER THERE MUST BE MY COACH.

THE BELL FOR THE LAST LAP!
DLEN
DLEN
DLEN
I HAVE TO...
...GIVE IT...
...MY ALL!

MEANWHILE, WILL...
YOU'RE MEETING THE TEAM FROM TAKESHITA AT 11. THEN YOU HAVE TO HURRY TO THE INAUGURATION OF THE NEW HEAD-QUARTERS. THEN...
MISS VANDOM? ARE YOU LISTENING?
I...YES, SORRY!
WHOA...THIS IS ME IN TEN YEARS. WHAT A RIDICULOUS HAIRSTYLE.
MISS VANDOM? MAY I PROCEED?
LOOKS LIKE I BECAME A BUSINESSWOMAN! NOOO! LIKE MY MOTHER!
HELLO? IT'S KATE, YOUR SECRETARY! I'M GOING THROUGH YOUR APPOINT-MENTS FOR TODAY.
UH, SORRY. DO CARRY ON.

AFTER THAT, YOU'RE MEETING THE NEW MANAGER FROM NEW YORK...
DO I EVER GET TIME TO REST?
THAT WOULD BE A FIRST! SHALL I WRITE IT DOWN?
DEFINITELY.
OKAY, REST! LET'S SAY HALF AN HOUR, AND AT 5 P.M., YOU COME BACK HERE. THE ADVERTISING TEAM NEEDS TO SHOW YOU THE NEW CAMPAIGN.
AT 7 P.M., A QUICK DINNER, AND AT 8 P.M...
UM...MY **BOYFRIEND** ISN'T IN THE SCHEDULE?
HA-HA! THAT'S HILARIOUS!
HA! YEAH! AND WE BOTH KNOW WHY, RIGHT?
BECAUSE AS YOU ALWAYS SAY, "I DON'T HAVE TIME FOR COFFEE, NEVER MIND A BOYFRIEND!"
HEH HEH...
HOW SCARY! WHAT HAVE I **BECOME**?!

AND WHAT AM I DOING NOW? MY MEMORY'S FAILING ME.
DLING
TESTING A NEW PRODUCT. THE BOARD OF DIRECTORS HAS BEEN SUMMONED, AS PER YOUR REQUEST.
ARGH!
G-GOOD MORNING.
ON BEHALF OF EVERYONE HERE, GOOD MORNING, MISS VANDOM.
WHAT SHOULD I DO? SMILE OR LOOK SERIOUS?
BOTH AT THE SAME TIME? A SERIOUS SMILE?
Look at that face. She's in a bad mood!
She's ALWAYS in a bad mood.

HERE'S THE NEW PRODUCT. I'VE BEEN INFORMED THAT THE **TASTE TESTERS** ARE ON THEIR WAY.
GREAT!
I GUESS?
AS USUAL, WE'D LIKE TO HEAR YOUR OPINION FIRST.
OF COURSE. ER...
THE COLOR LOOKS NICE.
BUT WHAT IS IT?
THE SMELL ISN'T BAD EITHER.
OUR TECHNICIANS DID THEIR BEST TO MAKE IT **ENTICING**.
OKAY, IT'S FOOD! OBVIOUSLY, IF THERE'S TASTING INVOLVED...
WE ADDED TAPIOCA FLOUR FOR EXTRA THICKNESS.
INTERESTING.

THE TEXTURE IS GOOD TOO.
I'M DOING AWESOME!
I'M GLAD YOU LIKE IT.
IT FEELS VELVETY. LIKE...A CARESS!
A CARESS! WE COULD USE THAT IN OUR ADS.
YEAH, WHY NOT? AS FOR THE TASTE...
AAAAH!
NOT BAD... MUNCH ...MAYBE IT'S MISSING A LITTLE PEPPER.
PEPPER?!

UM, YOU DIDN'T HAVE TO TASTE THE CAT FOOD, MISS VANDOM.
CHOMP
CAT FOOD?!
YES, HERE COME THE TESTERS.
MEOOOW...
PURR
OH! WHAT CAN I SAY EXCEPT...
PURR
...MEOW!
I think she needs a vacation!
Yeah, a LONG one!

WHAT ABOUT IRMA?
WHERE AM I?
IN A CLASSROOM? STILL? THAT MEANS...
...I FLUNKED AND FLUNKED AGAIN AND—
TEACH?
EXCUSE ME, TEACH? ARE YOU OKAY?
HUH? YES!
OH, I SEE.
I'M A TEACHER! GREAT!

ER...I GOT A BIT DISTRACTED. WHAT WAS I DOING?
YOU WERE ABOUT TO TAKE KATE TO THE PRINCIPAL, MISS LAIR.
RIGHT...THE PRINCIPAL.
SORRY 'BOUT THAT, KATE.
OKAY...I'LL LEAVE YOU ALONE FOR A MINUTE, BUT BEHAVE.
SHOULDN'T SOMEONE WRITE DOWN THE NAMES OF ANY TROUBLEMAKERS, MISS LAIR?
GOOD IDEA! I'LL LEAVE IT TO YOU.
YAY!
Why doesn't she bite her tongue?
LET'S GO, KATE.

BUT GO WHERE? I HAVE NO CLUE WHERE THE OFFICE IS.
I GOTTA FIND A WAY TO ASK WITHOUT BEING TOO OBVIOUS.
HEY, WHAT A SAD FACE...
WHY DON'T WE...SIT FOR A MINUTE?
WHATEVER YOU SAY, MISS LAIR.
YOUR EXPRESSION LOOKS FAMILIAR, SWEETIE...I'VE SEEN IT BEFORE.
YEAH?
YUP, IN MY OWN REFLECTION SOMETIMES!

LET'S SEE...TROUBLE AT HOME?
WELL...
"YES, A BIT."
TROUBLE WITH YOUR BOYFRIEND?
I DON'T HAVE A BOYFRIEND!
TONIGH
LOOKING
AND IS *THAT* TROUBLING YOU?
NO!
I MEAN...I *KINDA* HAVE A BOYFRIEND.
I GET IT—THE *DIFFICULT* TYPE.
"YEAH, DIFFICULT TO CATCH!"

ANYWAY, I'M USED TO IT. I ALWAYS END UP IN COMPLICATED RELATIONSHIPS.
THAT'S THE **ONLY** KIND THERE IS. YOU SHOULD KNOW THAT.
OF COURSE I KNOW. BUT I WON'T GIVE UP!
THAT'S THE SPIRIT. AND WHAT ABOUT AT HOME? IS IT **YELLING** OR **TEARS**?
A **MIX**...
COME ON, TELL ME.

...SO THAT'S WHAT HAPPENED. BUT IT COULD'VE BEEN WORSE, RIGHT?
FOR SURE.
DUM-DE-DUM...
YOU ROCK, MISS. THAT FELT LIKE TALKING WITH...**A GIRLFRIEND**!
OH, WELL... I AM PRETTY **YOUTHFUL**.
OKAY, LET'S HEAD BACK TO CLASS.
BUT... WHAT ABOUT THE PRINCIPAL'S OFFICE?
TO TELL THE TRUTH, I FORGOT WHERE IT IS.
LISTEN, BEFORE WE GO...DO YOU HAVE A MIRROR?
OF COURSE.

DARE I LOOK AT MYSELF, TEN YEARS OLDER?
YOU'RE NOT THAT BAD, TEACH. YOU CAN LOOK!
EH-HEH... RIGHT.
CUTE!
CUTE, YEAH?
NOW, LET'S GET TO CLASS. UM...WHAT WAS I EXPLAINING?
FRACTIONS!
UNBELIEVABLE, I'M A MATH TEACHER!
BY THE WAY, I DIDN'T UNDERSTAND PART OF THE FORMULA.
UH-OH! I GOTTA BUY TIME!
OKAY! BUT FIRST, GRAB A COFFEE WITH ME.

MEANWHILE, CORNELIA...
THIS IS MY FUTURE? I-IT'S HORRIBLE!
I LOOK AMAZING, THOUGH.
AND NO SPLIT ENDS!
BUT THESE BRIGHT LIGHTS ARE UNBEARABLE! NOT TO MENTION THE...
...VAMPIRE! AAAAAH!

AAAND CUT! WELL DONE, EVERYONE.
GREAT SCREAM, CORNELIA.
WOW! I'M SHOOTING A MOVIE!
YEAH, REAL BLOODCURDLING.
LIKE A STAR?
RECTOR
YOU WERE PERFECT AS USUAL, LEE.
SHALL I FIX YOUR MAKEUP?
NO!
SOMETHING TO DRINK?
NO! LEAVE ME ALONE WITH CORNELIA.
LISTEN, HONEY...
UGH! IS THIS MY BOYFRIEND?

...I'M THE STAR HERE! DON'T YOU FORGET THAT!
NOPE, NOT MY MAN.
YOU'RE JUST AN EXTRA. A NOBODY!
SO DON'T THINK YOU CAN STEAL MY SCENE. GOT IT?
HEY, FANG-FACE. LISTEN HERE—
I DON'T WANNA HEAR IT! GO GET ME A COFFEE!
ER...COME ON, CORNY.
BETTER PLAY ALONG. YOU KNOW HIM...HE COULD PULL THE PLUG ON THE WHOLE FILM.
YEAH?
COFFEE
BREAK
BRING HIM COFFEE WITH MILK AND SUGAR. HE'LL CALM DOWN AS USUAL.
ARE YOU SERIOUS?

I WONDER IF I'M STILL GOOD AT MAGIC IN THE FUTURE.
BIP
WELL, LET'S TRY...
COFFEE.
HMPH.
MAYBE YOU SHOULD REMOVE YOUR FAKE TEETH TO DRINK IT.
MAYBE YOU SHOULD SHUT UP.
AND MAYBE YOU SHOULD APOLOGIZE TO ME! I HAVE A SURPRISE FOR YOU...
!
MY TEETH ARE REAL... AND SO ARE MY SPIDERS!
WH-WHAT ...?

WH-WHERE'S THE DIRECTOR? WHERE'S THE CREW?
THEY'RE GONE... IT'S JUST YOU AND ME.
AND YOU KNOW, I'M FEELING THIRSTY. BUT IT'S NOT COFFEE I WANT...
AAAAH!
PLEASE, NO! NO! NO!
NOOOOOOO!
LEE? WHAT'S THE MATTER?
YOU'RE WORKING TOO HARD, LEE!
HUH? BUT...

SHE...SHE...SHE'S A WITCH!
DRINK YOUR COFFEE, LEE. UNLESS ...
...OOPS—YOU'D RATHER WEAR IT.
SPLASH
DANG, YOU'VE GOT GUTS!
GRR...!
That'll teach you to be rude.
AH!
HMM... I WONDER WHAT'S UP WITH...

...HAY LIN!
HUH, THAT'S IT? IN TEN YEARS, I'LL BE **GROCERY SHOPPING**?
AND LOOKS LIKE I'LL STILL BE IN HEATHERFIELD. THIS IS MY FAVORITE SHOE SHOP...
SALES
MISS LIN!
NEED A HAND?
UH...UM...NO THANKS.
HOW IS WORK?
ALL GOOD.
AT LEAST I HOPE SO!
YOU KNOW, MY ROSABEL JUST GRADUATED. I'M SO PROUD OF HER.
I'LL BET.

WELL, IT WAS NICE SEEING YOU.
HM? YOU'RE NOT COMING UP?
I AM! I WAS SAYING BYE EARLY, THAT'S ALL.
I GUESS I LIVE HERE.
I JUST GOTTA FIND OUT WHERE!
I HOPE THEY'LL FIX THE ELEVATOR SOON.
LUCKY YOU, LIVING ON THE LOWEST FLOOR.
BINGO!
HAVE A GOOD DAY, MISS LIN.
YOU TOO!
AND SAY HELLO TO YOUR HUSBAND FOR ME.
I'M MARRIED ?!

HI THERE, MISS LIN. HOPE YOUR DAY IS GOING WELL!
THANK YOU.
THE KEYS SHOULD BE IN MY POCKET...
HERE THEY ARE!
CLACK
I'M MARRIED, AND I HAVE LOVELY NEIGHBORS.
I'D SAY I'VE LEARNED ENOUGH ABOUT MY **FUTURE**.
GNEEK

I'LL JUST TAKE A LOOK AROUND AND...
WELCOME BACK, MISS LIN.
!
YOU'VE GOT MESSAGES. THEY CALLED FROM YOUR OFFICE. YOU HAFTA CALL BACK.
YOUR HUSBAND'LL BE HOME AT 5, AND HE'LL PICK UP THE DRY CLEANING ON THE WAY.
BY THE WAY, THERE'S A SMOOTHIE IN THE FRIDGE. I'M OFF—I'VE GOT SWIM CLASS TONIGHT.
OH, AND TESS WAS A DOLL, AS ALWAYS.

MOM! YOU'RE HOME!
BUT IT'S TIME TO RETURN...
WHATEVER YOU'RE DOING, IT'S TIME TO COME BACK.

SO? HOW WAS IT?
WELL...
IT WAS AWESOME! BUT I DON'T KNOW IF I WON AT THE OLYMPICS.
WELL, THAT'S WHAT YOU GET WITH A SNEAK PEEK...
TRUE, BUT I WOULD LIKE TO CHANGE THAT FUTURE A BIT.
DAAARLING!
IT'S POSSIBLE. PUSHING THE DOORS WILL RE-SHUFFLE YOUR DESTINY.
SOME THINGS WILL STAY THE SAME, AND SOME THINGS WILL CHANGE...
THEN I'LL RESHUFFLE!
TUMP

TUMP
HOW WAS YOUR FUTURE, WILL?
TUMP
COMPLICATED AND UNPLEASANT. I'LL RESHUFFLE!
TUMP
TUMP
TUMP
TUMP
ME TOO. I LIKED MINE, BUT I PREFER ***SURPRISES***.
TUMP
AGREED!
TUMP
AND YOU, HAY LIN?
I...

YOU'RE NOT GONNA RESHUFFLE?
NOPE!
WHY? WHAT DID YOU SEE?
I... I DIDN'T SEE IT CLEARLY...
"I DIDN'T SEE IT CLEARLY, BUT IT WAS BEAUTIFUL..."
THE END

YouWitch
Magical Moments to Experience Together!
Search
Closets
VIDEO
SEARCH
Posted by:
IRMA
Replay
Like
Great
Okay
So-So
Send to a Friend
Share
YOU'RE SO LUCKY, LETTUCE. I WISH I HAD A NICE SHELL LIKE YOURS...WEARING THE SAME OUTFIT ALL YOUR LIFE...
04:07 / 20:05 Closets
...INSTEAD, I GOTTA PICK ONE. UGH! WHY ISN'T THERE ANYTHING I LIKE?
IRMA? YOU READY? COME ON OUT. I WANT TO TRY MY NEW CAMERA.
NO! I'VE GOT NOTHING TO WEAR.
NOTHING...? HER CLOSET IS SO FULL, IT MIGHT EXPLODE.
KNOCK KNOCK

WOMEN ARE WEIRD SOMETIMES.
IS THAT SO?
YOU HAVE HUNDREDS OF SHOES AND DRESSES, BUT THEY'RE NEVER THE RIGHT ONES.
MEN, ON THE OTHER HAND...
I have three pairs of trousers and a few button-down shirts, honey. That's all I need.
BUT YOU OWN HUNDREDS OF SUCCULENTS, DON'T YOU?
WHAT'S THAT GOT TO DO WITH IT? THAT'S MY PASSION!
THE SAME GOES FOR MY CLOTHES!
AND HUNDREDS? WHAT A HYPERBOLE.
IT MAY BE... BUT WHAT'S THAT IN YOUR BAG?
ER...IT WAS HALF-PRICE!
THE SHOES I JUST BOUGHT WERE AS WELL.
QUIET! I CAN'T FOCUS!

FOCUS
FOCUS! THAT'S ALL YOU NEED TO MAKE A CHOICE.
IT'S USELESS. I'VE TRIED EVERYTHING!
I HAVE NOTHING TO WEAR.
LISTEN...I'LL TELL YOU MY SECRET METHOD.
PLEASE! PETER WILL BE HERE IN FIVE.
PICK AT RANDOM.
HUH?
CHOOSE RANDOMLY, GO TO THE BATHROOM, AND GET DRESSED. EYES CLOSED, NO MIRROR.
ARE YOU KIDDING?
TRUST ME— IT WORKS.
WELL...CAN'T HURT TO TRY.
GOOD!

I'M PUTTING IT ON WITHOUT LOOKING! **OW...** WHAT DID I HIT?
BE CAREFUL.
TUMP
VOILÀ! HOW IS IT?
AWFUL.
THEN WHAT DID YOU MAKE ME DO THAT FOR?
SO I'D HAVE TIME TO FIND YOU A NICE OUTFIT.
HERE...BLACK VELVET WITH A TOUCH OF SILVER.
P-PRETTY...BUT WHY DIDN'T YOU THINK OF IT SOONER?
WITH YOU YELLING AND PANICKING? IMPOSSIBLE. I TOLD YOU— YOU NEED TO ***FOCUS***.
YOU'RE A GENIUS! BUT NOW...***WHAT ABOUT MY HAIR***?!
HANG IN THERE... SHE'LL BE OUT OF THE HOUSE IN HALF AN HOUR.

SHOP CHOP-CHOP
I'VE GOT NOTHING TO WEAR!
TRUE...
WHAT?
IT'S TRUE! WE HAVEN'T BEEN OUT SHOPPING IN AGES.
THROW SOMETHING ON AND LET'S GO. HURRY, CHOP-CHOP!
GIMME A MINUTE! NO, HALF A MINUTE!
I'LL BE SUPER-FAST.
YANNO, MAMA...YOU STILL SURPRISE ME.
AS DO YOU. YOU'RE NOT WEARING SHOES!
UM...GIMME THIRTY MORE SECONDS.
SURE, BUT HOLD ON. I WANT TO TAKE A PHOTO!
CLICK

MINE, YOURS
COME ON, WILL... GET OUT OF THE CLOSET!
NO!
TOC TOC
IT'S NOT TRUE THAT YOU HAVE NOTHING TO WEAR. I'LL HELP YOU PICK A—
NO!
HMM...FINE, I'LL LET YOU LOOK IN *MY* CLOSET.
JUST LOOK?
NO, YOU CAN TAKE WHAT YOU WANT.
OKAY, I'M COMING!
SHAME WE'RE NOT THE SAME SHOE SIZE.
NOT *YET*...
TAC TAC TAC TAC TAC TAC TAC TAC

BIG NIGHT
I HAVE NOTHING TO WEAR.
OOH! CHECK THIS OUT...
SILK! IT'S A CLASSIC.
FOR THE ONE TIME DAD'S TAKING YOU OUT ...?
TRUE, HE PROMISED ME A BIG NIGHT.
WON'T IT BE TOO MUCH?
HIGH HEELS...
...CHUNKY NECKLACE...
...'80s-STYLE PURSE.
IT'S SO PRETTY! CAN I BORROW IT?
NO!

SO?
YOU LOOK GREAT!
GO CHECK IF DAD'S READY.
OKAY!
DAD— AH!
SO ARE WE READY?
HUH? WE'RE GOING WHERE?
THE PIZZA PLACE ON THE CORNER...
YOU CALL THAT A BIG NIGHT?!
RELAX... REMEMBER, HE'S YOUR HUSBAND! ALSO THE ONLY ONE WHO CAN OPEN JAM JARS...
I'M CHANGING, I'M CHANGING...
THE END

Read on in Volume 31!

W.i.t.c.h.
Will Irma Taranee Cornelia Hay Lin

Will
Irma
Taranee
Cornelia
Hay Lin

W.i.t.c.h.
Will
Irma
Taranee
Cornelia
Hay Lin

Part X. Ladies vs. W.I.T.C.H. • Volume 1

Series Created by Elisabetta Gnone
Comic Art Direction: Alessandro Barbucci, Barbara Canepa

JY
150 West 30th Street, 19th Floor
New York, NY 10001

Visit us at jyforkids.com
facebook.com/jyforkids
twitter.com/jyforkids
jyforkids.tumblr.com
instagram.com/jyforkids

First JY Edition: April 2023
Edited by Yen Press Editorial: Liz Marbach, Won Young Seo
Designed by Yen Press Design: Liz Parlett

JY is an imprint of Yen Press, LLC.
The JY name and logo are trademarks of Yen Press, LLC.

The publisher is not responsible for websites (or their content) that are not owned by the publisher.

Library of Congress Control Number: 2017950917

ISBNs:
978-1-9753-4469-6 (paperback)
978-1-9753-4470-2 (ebook)

10 9 8 7 6 5 4 3 2 1

LSC-C

Printed in the United States of America

Cover Art by Giada Perissinotto
Colors by Andrea Cagol

Translation by Linda Ghio and
Stephanie Dagg at Editing Zone
Lettering by Katie Blakeslee

ALL IN A DAY'S WORK

Concept and Script by Augusto Macchetto
Layout, Pencils, and Inks by Lucio Leoni

SUSAN AND DEAN'S WEDDING

Concept and Script by Augusto Macchetto
Layout and Pencils by Lucio Leoni

MUSIC IN THE AIR

Script by Teresa Radice
Layout by Giada Perissinotto
Pencils by Davide Baldoni
Inks by Marina Baggio and Roberta Zanotta

KITCHEN CATASTROPHES

Script by Augusto Macchetto
Layout and Pencils by Lucio Leoni

LADY GIGA

Script by Bruno Enna
Layout by Antonello Dalena
Pencils by Manuela Razzi
Inks by Marina Baggio and Roberta Zanotta

AN OWL AT THE WINDOW

Script by Augusto Macchetto
Layout and Pencils by Lucio Leoni

TEN YEARS LATER

Script by Augusto Macchetto
Layout by Giada Perissinotto
Pencils by Davide Baldoni
Inks by Marina Baggio and Roberta Zanotta

CLOSETS

Script by Augusto Macchetto
Layout and Pencils by Paolo Campinoti